Bound By Lies

Bound By Lies

The following is a work of fiction. Characters, names, situations,

events, and locations described in this novel are purely the invention of

the author's mind, or are used fictitiously. Any sort of resemblance to

people - living or dead, names and locations is purely coincidental. Any

references to real people, events, establishments

or locales are intended only to give the fiction a sense of reality and

authenticity. This story is copyrighted and cannot be taken or displayed

without the permission of the author.

Bound By Lies
By
Allison "Essence M" Edwards

Bound By Lies

Cover Concept and Design by Illuminnessence Publishing

& Dezigner Treatz

www. illuminnessencepublishing. com

Edited by Brandie Randolph / brandie@chicFABu. net

For all orders and inquiries, please contact

illuminnessencepub@gmail. com

Forever The Hustla- Chasing The Diamonds!!

Dedication

This book is dedicated to YOU!
You've stuck by my side on days when I felt I had
nothing left to give. When I cried myself to sleep at
night not knowing where the inspiration would come
from to complete this. On those days where nothing
seemed right and everything seemed wrong I
remembered that I have you. For that, I thank you. I
dedicate this book to LOVE.... You do exist and I
appreciate you in my life always!

Bound By Lies

Acknowledgements

First of all, I'd like to thank GOD for keeping me during some obstacles I've faced while writing this book. This is the second in a series that chronicles love and betrayal. The only one that gives unconditional LOVE is GOD and I learned that during this time.

Secondly, I'd like to thank my parents again. You've helped me in ways I can't even describe but I want to thank you publicly for being there when I needed you. My brothers and sister, you have given me inspiration beyond measure to do things that I never thought possible. I do it to show you that you can do it also.

My children, Jay and Mikey. I love you both, with all my heart and soul. You both are my reason for pursuing greatness and I see the same in you!

To those special friends that have TRULY supported me, I thank and love you! Y'all have been with me throughout the tears and the laughter. Thank you!

My author friends and acquaintances- Tanisha (Mahogani P) Pettiford, Shonda DeVaughn, Shannon Holmes, Tiphani Montgomery, Virginia Deberry & Donna Grant, Takerra Allen, Heather Covington, Erick Gray, Kaven Brown, CJ. Hudson, J. M Benjamin, K'wan, Shakeera Frazer, Anthony "KingPen AS" Moorer, Jackqueline "Boss Diva" Moorer, Dashawn Taylor ,Kisha Green, Kenya Mack, Keith Williams, Mo Shines, Novel Tees, Carla Dean, Kwame Teague, Tamika Newhouse, Lakia McDaniel, Nakea Murray, KD Harris, VJ Gotastory, Jason Poole, Charisse Washington, T. Styles and the rest of the Cartel Publications. I've learned so much from all of you and I thank you for the support you've given me. Love Ya!

To My Editor- Brandie Randolph, You have given my words life and have allowed them to breathe while I use the paper to hold the body. I thank you sincerely for sticking by me through the long period, for promoting me and for encouraging me to keep reaching for the stars and never stop dreaming! You Are SO FABU!!!

To my fans/supporters, I appreciate all the love you have given me as a newbie and I hope that you will continue to follow my journey. It's only the beginning of a journey that I plan to continue!

Whoever I "forgot", please know I love you still~Charge It To My Head and Not My Heart!

Much Love Always,

Allison "Essence M" Edwards

Bound By Lies

A Note from the Author

Welcome back to my journey. If you are reading this, then you have taken the time to purchase, or borrow my sophomore novel and for that, I thank you from the bottom of my heart! Initially this almost didn't come to fruition but did because of some very encouraging people most of whom I named in my Thank You's.

This novel takes you to a very different place but it still tells of secrets that are revealed when there's no communication and trust in a relationship. That holds true to all whether romantic or platonic. How can we want to be stronger in all aspects when we can't be real with ourselves?

I had to be real with myself in writing this and admit that love can be mistaken as lust and one needs to take a break, sit down and love themselves. After that, all will fall into place with God's help because HE is the be-all, end-all!

Once again, I thank you for continuing to read my works and I hope I can thrill you yet again. Your support is indelible and I love you all!

Allison "Essence M" Edwards
www. illuminnessencepublishing. com
illuminnessencepub@gmail. com

AFTER THE SMOKE CLEARS

The dark car that was previously parked up the street, screeched towards Lanai and Quincy. A piercing scream escaped from my lungs. The surrounding areas vibrated from the fatal collision. All that was left was smoke and exhaust. The assaulting vehicle vroomed off before I was able to get a look at the license plate or peer inside to see the offenders. I ran over to evaluate the damage and saw my husband and daughter laid out on the cement, suffering from a fatal hit and run. Who would do this to them? Were they really out to get me?

My heart palpitated in fear of the lingering results of the accident. I didn't know what to do, but I needed to get myself together for the sake of my family. I seemed to be the only one holding things together. Once the smoke cleared, I began to make necessary moves.

I looked over to my left and Rachelle dropped to the floor and began to cry. I didn't know if her tears were for herself or for genuine concern for Quincy. Quincy lay next to Lanai, bloodied and bruised, and she wasn't breathing. One of my neighbors had already called for medical assistance and I heard the sirens approaching in the distance soon thereafter.

I didn't move Q, but I placed his head gingerly in my lap and began to pray that all would be well.

"Oh, my God!" I yelled and Quincy whimpered in pain.

"Princess, is she, is she…okay?" he said, between breaths.

"Just stay still so they can tend to you," I said as I was unsure about the state of him or our daughter. As they loaded both of them into the ambulance, it looked grim for one of them.

Rachelle was sitting in her car with the kids and didn't know what to say or do. I ended up speaking for her.

"If you want to drive behind us, then that's fine. I'm going to be at the hospital regardless. My priority is my husband and child. You can do what the fuck you want at this point and, if I find out that you were behind this, I'm going to kill you!"Rachelle gasped and sobbed some more at my threat while I walked away and got into my royal blue Dodge Durango that Quincy had bought me for my last birthday.

As I entered the car and turned on the ignition, Mary J Blige's *No More Drama* came on the radio, prompting me to burst into a fit of tears. Just when I think things are getting better, they get just a tad bit worse.

I made several phone calls on the way to the hospital and everyone that needed to be there, arrived by the time I did, along with Quincy's mom and Malik, Quincy's best friend. The doctors worked feverishly with them and we all sat around, waiting. About two hours later, I was awakened by a soft hand in the lobby of the hospital waiting room. I grabbed my mother's hand, as well as my best friend Kaelyn's, who has stood by my side since the beginning. The doctors were ready to see me to give me the prognosis of my daughter and husband.

"Mrs. Thompson," the doctor said, "your husband suffered from a ruptured spleen, broken ribs, a broken leg, and a severe concussion. He may also have some short-term memory loss due to head trauma. We are going to suggest physical therapy for him and he'll be in the hospital for at least four weeks. "

"Oh, dear God!" I said, while tears ran down my face. "What about Lanai?" I asked. I wanted to know about my child's well-being.

The doctor's face said it all. "I'm sorry, Mrs. Thompson. We did all we could do, but her little heart couldn't withstand the trauma of her collapsed lung and she also suffered from broken ribs that punctured a vital internal artery. She started to bleed out, went into cardiac arrest, and eventually passed on. We will do all we can to help you at this difficult time. I'm so sorry for your loss."

The room began to spin and I felt feverishly hot all of a sudden. "Mrs. Thompson?" I heard the doctor say vaguely.

"AHHHHHHHHHHHHHHHHHHHHHHHHHHHHH H," I screamed until it all went black.

#####

MY OWN PERSONAL HELL

I heard myself yelling and jumped up. I thought it was all a dream but after I calmed myself and got my wits about me, I heard the rain beating against my windowsill in my bedroom. I felt like I was drugged and was sluggish and groggy. I felt like I had the weight of the world on my shoulders and I had no idea why. The only person right now that would be able to make me smile was somewhere, and I needed them.

"Lanai!" I called out to my daughter, waiting to hear her popular giggles and screams that always made me laugh when I needed her to.

"Lanai! Baby, come to Mommy and give her some sugar. " I know she is scared of thunder and lightning but I received no answer. I found that quite odd and began to get a weird feeling in my stomach. Just then, I heard someone walking up the stairs and I ran to the door and threw it open.

"Here's my lil' princess! Mommy missed you so much!" I said. Instantly, I felt puzzled because it wasn't who I wanted it to be.

"Quincy, where's our daughter? You know she's scared of thunder and lightning. Why are you leaving her to be by herself?" I demanded an answer about our "lost" child. Quincy looked at me with swollen red eyes and I noticed he was walking with a cane.

"Tamika, you need to rest and take something to sleep. It's been a long day,"he said, gently leading me towards the bed.

"What the fuck is wrong with you and why are you keeping me from my daughter? Why are you walking with a cane?" I was confused and began rambling off questions faster than he could answer.

Just then, the door opened and it was my mother.

"Miss Lorraine, she won't go back to sleep. She keeps resisting me," Quincy said. I noticed he and my mother both had the same look on their faces. It was sadness, grief, and helplessness. I then noticed their attire for the day. My mother had on a dark charcoal suit with white pearls and diamond hoops that were very simple, yet stylish. Her Tiffany solitaire necklace lay majestically on her white satin blouse. She didn't look a day past forty-five years of age, but was well up in her age at sixty-two. My mother took pride in her appearance and avoided stressful conditions as much as possible. It took her a long time to get to this point.

"Tamika, you must listen to Quincy and relax before you make yourself sick. " She gave him a weird look that almost was like a signal or something.

"Momma, I need to see my daughter! Where is she and why are you and Q acting like this?"She came over and gave me a hug. Quincy then gave me a kiss on the cheek and it was as if they both cleared the way for me to go downstairs, knowing that I'm the type of woman that does what she wants whenever she wants. I received clearance from my husband and my mother to see where my child was.

I descended the stairs and I heard a rumble of conversation. Some of the voices were fellow coworkers; my boss, Quincy's friends, and his mother were also present. My best friend, Kaelyn, was sitting in a corner holding a picture frame.

I recognized it as the frame containing a picture of her and Lanai when she was first born at her baptism. Everyone was dressed as my mom and husband were and they grew silent when I walked into the room.

"Hello, everyone. Why so glum?" I asked. No one responded and everyone had a puzzled look on their face. It wasn't until I looked down at my computer desk that I saw what seemed to be a program for a funeral. I'd not known anyone died. I looked at the picture on the front and it was Lanai. My hands froze and I flashbacked to the last couple of days. My baby was gone! It all came back to me like a tidal wave.

I remembered the car accident and I also remembered the argument with Rachelle. *Quincy was hurt in the accident as well*, I remembered.

I felt sick to my stomach and passed out on the living room floor. I felt arms around me and was given some water, along with a pill. My mother, who lay with me until I fell asleep, took me upstairs. There's nothing like a mother's love and I have nothing to show for my efforts of being a mom.

When I woke up, I was still in my bedroom. That's where I would be for the next few days, weeks, and months. Depression set in after I found out that my precious princess was gone. Lanai Kaelyn Adams-Thompson was laid to rest and she took a piece of me with her. She had just began to live life and I decided mine wasn't worth living without her. I spent a lot of time at home, reflecting what went wrong and how things would have been different. This went on for two months. My job as Marketing Director was still my sole form of employment. They were very understanding of the tragedy that took place, and I was given the option to work from home if needed. My grief from the loss of my daughter took a toll on me every day she wasn't with me. I remember when I finally snapped out of it...and snapped I did!

It was one Friday evening, and Quincy was on his way home from therapy. His progress was improving and he even felt well enough to try to initiate sex. I declined and he felt a bit rejected. I just wasn't in the mood to make love. . . not after losing Lanai.

One particular day, I woke up, knowing within myself that it was going to be a fucked up day. You know, one of those days where you just wake up and nothing seems to go right? It began with me almost losing my wedding band in the bathroom sink, but I caught it in time. Then I banged my toe coming down my stairs and ripped off my baby toenail. I decided that I needed to just crash on the living room couch and watch Oprah.

Right when I went to sit down, the phone rang. I hobbled over to get it and saw that it was my husband: **THOMPSON, QUIN** was listed on the caller ID.

"Hello," I said as I answered the phone. He was the only one that I would speak to and our conversations were very casual and dry.

"Hey, Tamika, I'm on my way home. Do you want to go out tonight?" He was trying to bring me out of my funk but it wasn't working. My response to him was silence. I stared at the TV and continued to listen to him. Nothing can change what happened and I regretted living each day I didn't have my daughter.

"I'll be home in about fifteen minutes. I'll bring some movies for us to watch and we'll relax, okay?"he said, trying to brighten my mood. It wasn't working and I just wanted yet another day to end.

"Whatever, Quincy," I answered him, without saying goodbye and placed the phone back in its cradle.

About ten minutes later, I was cuddled up in my favorite place in the house in the living room, which was the recliner. I was watching yet another episode of Oprah and the doorbell rang. I figured it was Quincy needing help at the door with food but it was a deliveryman.

"Afternoon, ma'am! I have a delivery for Mrs. Tamika Thompson," he said while holding a glass vase filled with multi-colored roses.

"I'll sign for it sir, thank you. " I signed my name on the delivery slip and tipped him ten dollars for his help. He smiled at me and then went back into his truck to continue his rounds. I closed the door behind me and began to feel a little warm. After Lanai's death, I had received so many bouquets and floral arrangements that I became sick and tired of them. Now it seemed as if these flowers came for a different reason.

I unwrapped the plastic covering and took a whiff of the wonderful aroma. I then noticed a card stapled to the plastic and removed it. I opened it and anger rose up in me.

It read: **An Eye for an Eye! Now You Know How It Feels To Lose Something.**

Just then, I heard the door open. It was Quincy, home from therapy.

"Hi, babygirl," he said, walking in sounding chipper and wanting so desperately to cheer me up. However, my back was turned and my face was stained with fresh tears. My clouded eyes turned towards the card in my hand that was written in mischief. Who would say such a thing? I can't deal with this bullshit again! I've had enough and I decided I wasn't going to take it anymore.

"Tamika, baby, I'm home," he repeated and just then, I turned around and responded by throwing the vase filled with flowers at him. He successfully ducked and it hit the wall, missing him by inches. Glass shattered everywhere and water spilled all over the carpet.

"What the fuck is wrong with you?" He was surprised by my reaction. Finally, I was able to reach down and tell him how I felt about all that had been going on.

"I want a divorce! Get your shit and get the fuck out!" I turned around and went back upstairs to my room to soak it all in.

"Tamika! What are you talking about?" He was in shock. After all we've been through, he never thought I would just give up like this.

I heard footsteps come up the stairs and Quincy gently touched me on the shoulder. I was lying on the bed clutching my pillow, with tears rapidly coming down my face. I was getting tired of dealing with this now and at a time when I needed him the most.

"Yes, Quincy! I meant what I said. You've lied to me for the majority of our relationship and I can't deal with it anymore. "

"Tamika, I've done nothing but come clean about everything! You know my family now and you know where

I work. I only see the kids with Rachelle when they come here. . . " I stopped him by holding up my hand.

"Q, do you know that Rachelle said she's pregnant with your child again? Have you seen her? She's about five months now because last I saw her was three months ago at the funeral. I told her if you died; I'd kill her. Our daughter died! Should I make good on my fucking promise?"

I was getting heated more and more by the moment, just thinking about it, and was silently making plans on how to get rid of the problem. I then realized that the baby didn't have anything to do with it. It was Quincy, yet again, that was the root of the problem.

I continued my rant," she told me you were the father of her baby; that you were still sleeping with her and that's what we were fighting about when Lanai got hit by the car. I'm tired of fighting your battles and losing. I love you and our child so much and I lost everything. I lost my sanity; I don't trust you anymore and Lanai is gone! What am I supposed to do now? Please tell me how I am supposed to go on knowing that my family is gone! Your family with Rachelle is what you have. You have no life with me! Lanai is all I had and she's gone!"I began sobbing until my chest heaved up and down. It was a gut-wrenching cry that existed and originated in the depths of my loins.

"It's okay, baby! I love you! I'm sorry! I will deal with Rachelle! I know a lot is my fault! I did all this and, as God is my witness, I promise we will get through this!" Quincy held me closely and didn't let me go for the rest of the night. We both slept in each other's arms. I was hurt, but I did love him- just not enough to let go yet. I realized silently that I was speaking in anger, and the only way I could truly get over it was to make him feel the pain that I did. I decided to sleep on my decision of leaving him and concoct a plan filled with vengeance. He wasn't going to get away scot-free.

When I woke up the next morning, Quincy was still asleep with his head on my chest. His eyes were beet-red and swollen. After seeing him, I felt bad because I never really gave him a chance to grieve our child. I just took every opportunity to beat him into the ground as if he hadn't lost a baby, too.

I eased from under him, slowly, and went to the bathroom to wash my face. I had nowhere to go, but my spirit was so broken. I splashed some water on my face and looked up at my reflection. I was a shadow of my former self and I needed to change that. My dark brown hair was in a ponytail and hadn't been combed for days. My dark eyes showed the lack of sleep that I hadn't received for almost three months.

I needed to get back into the swing of things and I was going to begin now. I took the rubber band out of my hair, combed, and brushed it. I then turned on the shower and when I came out in just a towel, I felt like me again. I exited the bathroom and went back into the bedroom. When I entered, I heard Quincy whispering on the phone with his back turned.

"No, she has no idea. I can't tell her that. Hell no! Yeah! I'll call you later to check on the progress. No problem. Thanks!" He ended the call and was somewhat shocked when he turned around to see me standing there.

"More secrets, Quincy? Damn! When are we going to get past all the lies? I thought we could go through Lanai's death together. I know you are dealing with your own loss but I'm still trying to figure out who the hell sent the flowers and also who tried to kill you and successfully got to Lanai. " I started getting angry again.

"I don't know what to tell you, Tamika. I'm sorry, but I don't. Maybe it's some old dude that you used to deal with. You've got enough of those lying around. Speaking of which, Trevor called to see how you were. " Quincy rolled his eyes as he gave me the message.

"I know you're not throwing blame at me when you had some bitch follow me all around New York City and even come to my house! Rachelle will forever be a thorn in my side! You know what? I was thinking that things could work out between us but maybe it's best we just separate for a little while, until we figure out how to co-exist. Blaming each other isn't going to bring our daughter back," I said while staring at Quincy with piercing eyes.

Quincy angrily got up from the bed and grabbed his overnight bag.

"You just may be right. I'll get some things and go stay with my mom. If you need me, please let me know and know that I love you. I didn't want us to have to do this, but it may be best. " Quincy walked away from me and sat on the bed.

Quincy threw enough clothes in the bag for a few days and zipped it up. He walked over and kissed me on the forehead. He did that the first day I met him, too, and that was our little thing we had. I know within my heart that I was pushing him away but I needed to forgive him before I was able to move on and, right now, I didn't think I could.

"Where will you go, Quincy?" I wanted to know where he was going. He's still my husband and I still cared.

He looked at me with a look like *why the hell should you care?*

"I'm going to stay with my mother in the Bronx. I also need to get my mind right. I love you with all my heart and you need to learn to trust me, but I need to figure out what to do with Rachelle. She's tearing us apart slowly but I need to take care of home first. "

"Take care of home? Who the fuck were you talking to when was in the shower? You are still keeping secrets from me! How can you take care of home when you are sitting up in our home, lying to my face about who you know and what you are doing?" I began to rant and rave all over again.

I decided to make some phone calls and get back to the land of the living. First, my mother and father called, and I knew I had to speak to them. They had called me every day and I told Quincy to tell them I was asleep.

"Hi, Mom," I said as she answered on the second ring.

"Tamika? Hey, snookums!I was praying for you a few minutes ago! How are you feeling?"

"I feel like shit, but I'm working on it. " I thought about telling my mom that Quincy and I separated but decided against it.

"I understand what you mean, but you must at least visit her site to get over the pain. Your father and I went a few days ago and it helped us a little by remembering her life-as short as it was. I laughed as I remembered when she tried on my glasses that day and…"

"Tamika, are you there? I said your father and I are going to go see Lanai's gravesite tomorrow. We can swing by and pick you up if you want. . . "I zoned out but came back to reality when I realized that she was trying to force me to go to the gravesite. I cut my mom's thought off abruptly.

"Mom, I have to go. I'll call you later, okay? Love you! Bye!"

I hung up the phone before she could change my mind and I began to sob. The loss of our daughter was something I don't know if I could deal with. It will be a daily struggle.

The phone jolted me out of my thoughts. I was still crying when I answered, sure that it was my mom attempting to convince me about the next day's field trip.

"No, Mom, I'm not going!" I picked up the phone and simply said.

"Hi, Tamika. I'm not going either, but if you want me to, I can," said the voice on the other end of the line. It wasn't my mom. It was Trevor, my ex-boyfriend.

#####

A SHOULDER TO LEAN ON

"Hello," said Trevor. I was very surprised to hear from him. He kept his distance from me after he saw me about a year ago. I still didn't know what to say to him but I'm sure he didn't know what to say to me, either.

"Trevor? Hello! How are you?" I said as I sat on the edge of my bed.

"I'm good, Tamika. I actually wanted to contact you a while ago but then I heard about your daughter, and I extend my condolences again. " He sounded so somber. When he and I were together, we were expecting, but I lost our baby. He always wanted children but our timing was a bit off and after our relationship ended, I threw myself into work.

"Thank you, Trevor. My husband and I appreciate it. " As soon as I said that, I regretted it.

"How is Quincy?" Trevor asked inquisitively. I didn't know how to respond but no one needed to know we were going through problems. Trevor, however, caught me.

"We're managing as best we can. Our daughter's death has taken a toll on our marriage, so we decided on a brief separation". A single tear fell from my face and I didn't know if it was for Lanai, or for my marriage that was clearly falling apart.

Why was I divulging all information to someone that was from my past? I don't know. Surely, he has an ulterior motive and will use it against me. I'll just have to wait and see.

"Tamika, are you there?" I heard Trevor say.

"Huh? I'm sorry Trevor. I zoned out for a second. I'm getting prepared to go to the mall. " I threw on some jeans, a V-neck sweater, and some boots. It was between seasons and I didn't know how to dress, but I knew I had been cooped up in the house way too long. I needed to get out and about.

"Which mall are you going to? I was going to do some shopping and was going to The Galleria. I can meet you there for Starbucks if you like?" Trevor was always charming and I needed to vent to someone, so, I agreed.

"Okay. I'm dressed and will meet you there in thirty minutes," I said as I grabbed my beige Coach purse and my keys.

I locked up everything and grabbed the house phone replacing it in the cradle. With my keys and my Blackberry in hand, I headed out to the truck and realized my blue Durango was dirty! I hadn't washed her in weeks but, then again, I hadn't been in the mood to do anything in months.

As I opened the car door, my Blackberry rang, and it was Quincy. I answered it, noticing that there were wilted roses on my car seat.

"Hey, Quincy," I said, between pauses. I was swallowing tears of mental exhaustion.

"Tamika, what's wrong? And don't tell me nothing!" He was getting nervous.

"I'm okay. I just got in the car and I saw some roses in there and I think I'm being stalked again. I can't take this shit anymore. We just lost Lanai and I lost you and I damn near lost my mind. . . " Quincy interrupted me.

"Baby, remember a few days ago when I wanted us to go out to dinner? I put those in the car for you to see, but then you spazzed out on me. "

I felt like such a fool. They were lovely but half-dead, just like what my life had become. This grief was becoming overwhelming, and more than I could bear, if I wasn't careful.

"I'm so sorry, Q. We'll talk when I get back home. "
I still had an appointment to keep with Trevor and was
running late.

"Where are you off to?" I didn't want to lie to him
but his questions kept coming. I felt obligated to tell him
the truth, but it would hurt too much and appear that I was
seeking comfort in the arms of another man.

"I'm going to the mall in Queens. They have a great
spa and I'm going to pamper myself. I've been looking and
feeling like shit and I've been holding on to that spa
certificate ever since Lanai was born. " I hoped that it didn't
sound too farfetched.

"All the way in Queens? Why not stay in
Westchester?" Quincy kept prodding and holding me up. I
had to make this believable, even though I wasn't doing
anything wrong.

"Quincy, I'm not staying around here. Everything I do reminds me of the baby, and of you. The ice cream parlor, the toy store, at home I still smell her baby blanket. I need to heal and I need to do things that will help me move on. "

There was a long pause and I heard sniffing. This was getting to him.

"Q, I'll call you when I get back and we will have dinner and I'll show off my new 'do. You can come by the house, okay? Love you. "

"I love you too, Midnight! We'll get through this!" Quincy hadn't called me that in a long time. I knew I had slipped up by telling him I loved him, but that's how I felt, and will always feel, for my husband.

I ended the call and started the car to make my way to the mall. By the time I got to Starbucks, Trevor was already there with packages, and I was fifteen minutes late.

"Hey, Trevor," I called out to him, almost out of breath.

"Hey, Tamika, no worries. You are just in time. I took the liberty of ordering for you. A caramel macchiato with extra whip cream right?" He knew that was my weakness and I was a creature of habit when it came to coffee. I cut down on it after we broke up.

"Thank you, Trev. " I smiled and sat down to take a sip. It warmed my insides and I wondered if it was the attention, or if I was actually feeling something for another man.

"Anytime, so tell me how you've been. I've been working hard as project manager to get Kinko's back on the map. Many people have been going with Staples. That's kind of what I wanted to talk to you about. I know your firm handles a lot of accounts and I wanted to know if they wanted to take on Kinko's as well. " Trevor continued to pitch his idea and the more I listened, the more I became pissed off.

"Trevor, you brought me out of my house and told me you wanted to talk to me about life and my child with the ulterior motive to pitch work shit to me? I've not been to work in almost three months. I work from home and I'm still dealing with my daughter's death! You've got a lot of nerve!" I was beyond pissed now and I didn't even drink my coffee.

"Tamika, I wanted to talk to you about your daughter, too. I sent you a wreath. I also remembered how you reacted to me when I last saw you and I guess I wanted to show you that I was doing more than being a copy boy. I know that's what you thought when you saw me last but, honestly, I am the Regional Manager of the Finance Department and my position is to find clients that are willing to invest in our company's marketing strategies that will secure revenue for both you and the client. I'm managing something positive and I hoped you would be proud of me," he said, looking like a little boy.

I grabbed the chair once again and sat down. I felt used.

"Trevor, I appreciate you trying to prove something to me, but you don't have to. I am a married woman grieving over a child that I just lost. If anything, just show support," I said as I wiped my face. I've been doing more crying than anything the last few days and it was getting annoying. After all that's happened to me, dating back from college, I had decided not to cry. But, lately, it was becoming more difficult.

"Where's your support system? I don't see him here with you. You've done nothing but ignore your husband's phone calls since I've been here and I know you and him are going through problems. The one person that's here for you and you shit on them. Now, either sit and listen, or be on your way. You underestimate my love for you. " Trevor was getting annoyed at my responses to him and I was getting equally aggravated with him pretending to care about me and my daughter.

"Oh, really? You are here for me? It's funny how, now, you are all of a sudden supportive. When I had to terminate our child because you refused to be there for

me when I needed you-was that supportive? When I had to sell some of my things to pay for my procedure because you took my name off of all of our joint accounts because, as you say you were on the way out the door anyway'-was that supportive? I mean, yes, I know we were struggling and breaking up, but, damn. That was your baby and you just abandoned me. It was then that I realized that I needed to get my shit together and do for me because you weren't going to be there for me when I needed you. "

I was beginning to cause a scene and everyone was looking at us. Trevor grabbed my arm and attempted to silence me. I glared at him.

"Tamika, you are causing people to look at us like I'm hurting you. " Trevor placed his arm gingerly through my arm and guided me out of the Starbucks and into the parking lot.

I snatched my hand away and glared at him. "Trevor, you are hurting me!" I hissed at him. I looked around and noticed everyone staring and whispering.

"You know what; maybe this isn't a good time for us to speak. I've got some unresolved feelings concerning our relationship and now is not a good time for us to discuss them. I feel as if this has only opened old wounds. "

I searched through my bag for a tissue and it tumbled out of my hand, along with all of the contents, dispersing onto the sidewalk. Trevor bent down to assist me in picking them up.

"I'm such a fucking klutz. I haven't been myself in months. I just need to get my life back together. " I was now sobbing uncontrollably, something I was used to doing at any given moment. Trevor found a tissue and handed it to me while guiding me to my car.

"Thank you, Trevor. I've not been right the last few days especially. I just feel like everyone is against me for some reason or the other. I'm not insecure; I'm just afraid and I shouldn't be," I said, revealing my inner feelings to Trevor. He was always a good listener but this time, I wanted more. We stopped by my car and I looked up into his eyes. He seemed genuinely happy to see me and that he was able to calm me down. Surprisingly, I was also, and I leaned up to give him a kiss on the cheek.

It was a sensual kiss and lead to more. I kissed the side of his lips and then we looked at each other with unbridled passion. It was clear we were both seeking something from the other. He held me closely and kissed me gingerly on the lips, sliding his tongue deep within to dance with mine. I responded by gasping and ingesting his spirit within mine. Outside of the car, we stood as if nothing else mattered but us, and we had to catch ourselves.

"Trev, we need to stop! Things won't change for us," I said. I was worried that we wouldn't be able to stop once we began.

"Tammy, I'm here for you. You know this. . . give me a call so we can talk, because we still have ties to clear up and I still want to work with you regarding the business proposition. "

"Trevor, we'll be in touch. I have to get home and work things out. Today has been a crazy day!" I grazed his cheek with my hand and got into my car. My hands were on the steering wheel and shaking uncontrollably. I knew that my integrity and loyalty will be questioned and I had to make sure that I was making the right decision. I decided that, ultimately, what Q didn't know wouldn't hurt him. As much as Quincy has hurt me in the past, I can afford to keep a secret from him.

I mean, he kept so much from me for years. I wiped my face, started my ignition, and my Blackberry rang. It was Quincy calling me. I had to let him know that I didn't make my spa appointment and was much closer than he thought.

"Hello," I said, as I got on 95 North. Good thing I had a Bluetooth because I couldn't hold the phone and drive at the same time.

"Hey, Mika, everything okay?"

My guilt for that kiss was taking over and I began stuttering.

"Hey, Q, uh, yeah. . . I am okay. Why do you ask?" I said, as I tried to regain some normalcy in my voice and demeanor.

"I just wanted to make sure you were. I'm leaving work to go to therapy and wanted to know if you wanted to get dinner and talk. We have to think about what we plan on doing. I don't want to lose you again. "

I knew where he was going with this, but I couldn't not let him at least try. We had both invested so much into the relationship, but I was tired of the back and forth. Unless we fixed it, nothing would change.

"Okay. I'll meet you at home and we can leave all our cares behind tonight. We will play it by ear," I said, agreeing to dinner and a night of relaxation with my husband.

EMOTIONAL ROLLERCOASTER

I gathered my things and pulled up to our home thirty minutes later. There was no sign of Quincy. I decided I was going to get myself together so we could just leave when he got here, depending on how long it took him to get ready. He hated waiting on me but I think this time would be different. I dropped my purse on the couch and walked up the stairs to the bedroom. When I walked in, I saw the bed freshly made and rose petals all over it. On the nightstand, there was a single rose, which said:

Let Us Get Back All That Was Lost, Let's Take It Back To the Beginning. . . Love Q

I found a silk robe on the bed and decided that, since I was going to take a shower anyway, I would change into the robe, and then I walked into the bathroom. I opened the door to find our bathroom surrounded by candles and a bath drawn. I bent down to feel the water and it was still steaming hot so I surmised that it had been drawn recently. The last time Quincy was this romantic was when I was pregnant with Lanai. I decided to step into this bath and indulge in all that was provided for me.

I removed my robe and stepped one foot in, followed by the other. It felt so nice and warm. As I immersed my whole body into the bath, I touched it with my hand to discover that it's a milk bath with rose petals floating inside. I gently sat in the tub and thought of how good it felt. I sit there, for what seems like forever, and I begin to hear music playing. It sounds like Jill Scott or Maxwell and it begins to come closer and closer.

Soon, I look up to see Quincy, standing in the doorway with an old-school boom box. In its tape deck is "Just Me and You" by Tone, Toni, Tony. I loved that song when it first came out and it fit how I felt at the moment. Right now, nothing else mattered but Quincy and me.

Quincy came into the bathroom and placed the radio on the toilet seat. He leaves again and comes back with two glasses and a bottle of Moscato. We had a bottle of it at our wedding and we had the best time. He wasn't playing when he said he wanted to make things like it used to be. He poured a glass for me, and then for himself, and sat on the edge of the bathtub.

"I love you, Tamika!" Quincy said to me, as he toasted the glass to me. I looked at him in total surprise and shyness. It's been so long since he catered to me like this. I know it was because he wanted to show me how sorry he was for everything. Stress totally took over our life for the last few months and we forgot who we were to each other.

"I love you too, Quincy. This is such a welcomed surprise. I didn't expect this at all, and it feels very good. " I took a sip and Quincy took my glass. He turned on the faucet and set it to warm, while adding soothing bubble bath carefully, making it so that it didn't run over. He reached down into the bathtub and grabbed my right foot. My toes still had the French manicure design on them and Quincy loves my feet. I think they're all right, but he adores them. He always had a foot and shoe fetish, and this time was no different.

"Q, what are you doing to me?" I chuckled as he kissed each and every one of my toes until he got to my big toe. He placed my big toe in his mouth and sucked it slowly and sensually. I moaned in delight for I haven't felt this type of arousal in weeks, months even.

Quincy looked at me knowingly and asked, "do you like how this feels?" He already knew my answer, but he wanted to make sure. He slowly placed my foot back in the bathtub and came to sit at the head of it. He moved the bath pillow and placed it so that it was leaning on him, and I placed my head there. He reached down, began to massage my shoulders slowly, and moved the bubbles to expose my round, chocolate breasts.

Surprisingly, he found my nipples erect from the sensual contact. I moaned in pleasure as he tweaked them and I slid lower into the water, allowing the warmth to take over my body. I couldn't take it anymore and began to feel tingling in regions that I'd not felt in a long time. I didn't know how to react to it, and he knew it.

"Baby, you feeling okay? Do you want me to stop?" Quincy asked.

By this time, he had traveled back down to my legs and was rubbing my stomach and between my legs. He knew what he was doing and it was working. I held up my hand to have him assist me out of the tub and he greeted me with a huge, plush, emerald-green bathrobe. He knows that's my favorite color and it felt so warm. Quincy led me to the bedroom and placed me gingerly on the bed, drying me off completely with the matching emerald-green bath towel.

"Quincy, what is it that you are doing to me and why?" I asked, and had more questions, but he silenced me with a simple kiss to my lips. I knew then that he would show me more than he would tell me. Quincy laid me gingerly on the bed, began to rub my feet slowly, and placed a kiss on each one of my toes, ending it by sucking my big toe passionately. He kissed my feet and I moaned seductively. I've never had that done before and it felt so good. I reached up and grabbed my breasts to feel my nipples become erect at his warm tongue, licking my toes slowly and sensually.

I reached up, grabbed his face, and began kissing him passionately, loving the feeling that I was experiencing. It had been a while since I was able to make love without thinking of things pertaining to our past, but

Quincy made it very simple to do. He removed the towel and slowly began kissing my neck, breasts, and stomach. I moaned and began to feel warm in regions that I had not felt a thing in months. Quincy took each one of my fingers and began kissing them slowly and then realized that I was still wearing my wedding band and engagement ring.

"You're still wearing your ring!" Quincy said, surprised. He knew I was ready to serve him divorce papers after our last blowup, but he's still my husband, regardless.

"Yes, why wouldn't I? You are still my husband," I responded, as if reading his mind. I gently kissed his lips slowly, while placing my hands in his baggy jeans. I felt his erection through his boxers and was eager to make love to him.

"Midnight, I want you," he whispered in my ear, kissing me simultaneously. I pulled the zipper on his jeans and began tugging on them, slowly releasing the hold. Quincy stood up and removed his Timberland boots and socks. He removed his Polo shirt, dropped it in a pile on the floor, and began to kiss my pussy slowly. My walls contracted at the touch of his tongue and I moved slowly beneath him, grabbing the rungs on the headboard for support. His tongue slowly lapped up whatever juices I emitted from my leaking vagina. I was ready to receive him and I wanted him now.

His massive erection was poking through his boxers and I pulled them down with my hands while he straddled me. I began to kiss his lips and tasted myself, which turned me on even more.

"Q, make love to me now!" That's all I could muster before he entered me with deep thrusts. He grunted while he straddled me and spread my legs so wide that I felt him deep within my gut. With every pounding thrust, I heard

Quincy say, "I love you," and I knew that was a feeling that he would always have, no matter what. My mother always said, "just because a man loves you, doesn't mean it's how you need to be loved," and I have to remember that's the only way he knows how. I held that piece of knowledge with me and always remembered it. Maybe that's why I held onto Quincy's bullshit so long.

His wet tongue entered my mouth and interrupted my thoughts, causing me to focus on the feeling he was giving me. He kissed me passionately, placed my right leg on his left shoulder and began thrusting hard, his chocolate dick throbbing inside of me. My clit responded to the feeling, my panting became very heavy and labored, and I began to respond accordingly. I felt his fingers begin to play aggressively with my black pearl and I knew I was reaching climax. Back and forth, he rubbed it until it began to have a life of its own. My pussy was waiting to drench his dick with my juices and I was ready to receive his loving.

"Oh, yes, Quincy! Damn, baby! Give it to me!" I said, moaning uncontrollably. All the sex we've not had built up to tonight, and it was well worth it. My nipples began to tingle at the feel of him inside of me and I knew I couldn't manage it much longer. I was tight and wet, and the deeper he went, the more I felt myself about to cum.

"You like it, baby? Take it! This is yours! All yours! God, I love you! Arghhhhhhhhhhhhhhhhhhhh!"

Quincy's hot, milky syrup ejected itself into my canal and I accepted it all. We both lay, spent, on the bed and his phone vibrated on the nightstand. I looked at him and he looked at me.

"Aren't you going to get that like you normally do? It might be business," I said. I was just waiting for him to up and leave me like he usually does and I felt that this wasn't any different. He proved me wrong.

"No, Baby! Tonight, it's all about you and I want to spend the night with you if I can. "

I was shocked and amazed that he wanted to do even that, but I decided to agree because I knew this night was too good to be true. The last time I felt like that, I was right!

"Oh, okay. I didn't want to take you away from anything that was pending," I said, as I stroked his chest that I was now laying on. After an evening of passionate lovemaking, I felt more comfortable than ever with him, but I was still on guard. It was 11:30pm.

We had both fallen asleep when I heard vibrations coming from his coat pocket. I was trying not to be *that woman* that searched her man's pocket, but after what we went through, I couldn't be too sure. I slowly crawled from beneath him and he moaned softly. It seemed that all that lovemaking wore him. I quietly tiptoed over to his jacket and stuck my hand in his inside pocket. In it, I found another phone, but this one was a Blackberry. I shook my head and just looked at it. Why does he have another phone? Just as I decided to leave well enough alone and place the phone back into his pocket, the phone vibrated in my hand. On the screen appeared the name and number of **Jazmine -347-555-8274.**

The Tamika I want to be didn't answer it, but the Tamika I've become copied the number and sent a text with it from his phone to mine. I was positive that it would come up again and, this time, I would be more than ready.

I crawled back into bed and began to think of my method of action concerning my husband. I also realized that we didn't use any protection during our session of lovemaking. That, along with other things, would have to be addressed when we woke up the next morning.

A DISH SERVED COLD

The following morning, after we spent the night together, became the first day in a long time that we actually were a married couple. I woke up, smiling for several reasons, and they all had to do with Quincy. For the most part, I was still in love with him and we definitely shared history. However, most of that history was based on lies and dishonesty, so I was determined to keep my guard up. I decided to continue to learn more about Quincy by playing his game. After all, he was always interested in playing games, but I learned over time that to play the game, you don't just participate…you play to WIN!

I sat up in bed and looked at my surroundings. Quincy was up and about, and I looked over at the clock. It was 9:47am and I was shocked to know it was so early. It was a Saturday morning and I felt better than I had felt in a long time. Thoughts of Lanai ran through my head and I knew that, on a day like this, we would go shopping and go for ice cream. I began to tear up at the thought of my only child gone way too soon, but I smiled at the time we spent. I picked up a picture of the three of us that rested on my nightstand. We were so happy as a family, despite all that drama. I wanted that life back. As a matter of fact, I wanted MY life back, and today was the day I was going to do it.

I hopped out of bed and went downstairs, into the bathroom. The candles from last night had burned out and the soap in the bathtub left a residue around the tub. The radio was still playing its harmonious tune of soft music that began everything and I replayed how it made me feel. I smiled and brushed my teeth, holding my long ponytail behind me as I spit the toothpaste into the sink. I washed my face, mouth, and hands, and lifted my head to wipe my face. As I looked up, I saw Quincy's reflection behind me in the mirror and screamed.

"What the hell?" I said, wiping my face with a hand towel and regaining my composure.

"Hey, Baby! I am sorry I scared you. Are you okay?" he said, as he placed his hand around my waist and kissed me on the forehead.

"I'm fine," I said, trying to convince him, as well as myself, that my outward appearance mirrored my inward. I was a little uneasy but I decided to make the best of it.

"Let's go, Baby. We're going to have a fun-filled day for you and I. " Quincy was happy to be dedicating all this time to me and I was surprised at the gesture.

"We are? Why? And how should I dress?"I wanted to throw on my usual sweats and a wife beater but I knew he'd want me to dress up.

"Pick something cute. I want us to go to breakfast and then spend the day in the city. "

I decided to just go with the flow and actually give him something to look forward to. I ran upstairs to my closet and looked for, what could possibly be, the perfect outfit. I settled on a light blue sundress, a sweater, and some espadrilles. I had my long, brown hair in a ponytail, but removed it and let my long, flowing curls frame my heart-shaped face. I grabbed my makeup and applied liner, mascara, and lip-gloss to finish it off. I was looking cute and I knew it.

Forty-five minutes later, I skipped down the stairs and saw Quincy staring at me, while he stood at the foot of the banister. He hadn't seen me looking like that in a while and was pleasantly surprised.

"Damn, Baby! You look so sexy right now. I changed my mind. We don't have to go out. Let's stay in and continue what we started last night," he said, as he ran his fingers up the side of my thighs. I knew exactly what he meant and that reminded me of what occurred last night when we made love without using any form of protection.

I took his hand and guided it slowly away from my legs, and my face showed how annoyed I was. We used no barrier between us and he's getting phone calls from other women-STILL. Not to mention, we have Rachelle with another one of his children. This marriage is becoming less than worth my while, but Quincy is going to tie up each and every loose end before things get too crazy.

"Baby, what's wrong? You don't want any more of my loving?" Quincy said, apparently because of my reaction to him touching me. I wanted him to understand my discomfort.

"Quincy, first of all, we just started to heal over the loss of Lanai. I don't think I could handle another pregnancy and, furthermore, we are not stable enough emotionally to raise another child. You have two children with Rachelle, one on the way, and child support is whooping your ass. Do you think you could handle another child? I mean, I'm going back to work soon and then I'm thinking of venturing it out on my own and beginning my own business. That's going to conflict with everything we are trying to rebuild, don't you think?" I was getting angrier the more I thought about the fact that Rachelle has children for him, but I have nothing.

Quincy looked at me silently and just walked away. I thought he was going to come back, but I heard the ignition start and the car disappeared down our street. I walked over to the window and saw the car fade into the sunlight and wondered if Quincy had had enough this time. One part of me cared and then the next part absolutely didn't, because I was still angry with him. I realized that he wasn't coming back anytime soon when I sat for an hour, flipping channels. I decided to just clear my thoughts and get something to eat. Just then, the phone rang and I hoped it was him, but it was my best friend, Kaelyn.

"Well, look what the cat dragged in," I said, without even answering the phone with a "hello".

"Bitch, please! You are living up in suburbia and we have to suffer and live in the 'hood," she said, with a hearty laugh. Kaelyn and I haven't spoken in a few weeks, but that was still my best friend.

"How are you doing, missy?" Kaelyn asked, sounding somber, and I knew she was thinking of how I was dealing with Lanai's death. I was missing in action for a little while and Kaelyn loved me enough to let me mourn.

"I'm managing, chica! Taking it one day at a time and it's very hard, but Quincy is trying his best to help. We actually had a good weekend. " I didn't mention that he and

I just had an argument about kids and Rachelle. Sometimes, it's best to not say it all, and I was tired of airing my dirty laundry.

"Aww, your godson, Javon's, birthday is tomorrow. Are you still coming to his birthday party? You know I agreed that, after seven years old, he will have no more parties and this one is at Chucky Cheese. "

"Yeah, I'll come, and I'll bring some of his gifts. The rest of them I'll come over with Quincy, so he can show him what he got him. " I paused for a moment, wondering if Quincy was even coming back. As soon as I did, the other line on the phone clicked.

"Kae, hold on. . . I've got to take the other line," I said, and then clicked over to the other line.

"Hello," I said, anxiously. I hadn't been in the habit of answering the phone, but I figured it was safe this time.

"Tamika, it's me. I'm at the hospital," Quincy said.

NOTHING BUT TROUBLE

"Baby, I'm sorry about what happened earlier. I'm just frustrated at how my life has turned out and, even more so, our life. Wait! Did you say 'at the hospital'? Are you okay?"I started to panic at the thought of being at a hospital again and losing someone near and dear to me.

"Quincy, I just want you to tell me what happened now! I can't take too much more of this!"I began to yell at him through the phone.

"Rachelle is having the baby. I left home to clear my mind and I got a phone call. I thought it was you and I answered. Come to find out, Rachelle is going to have the baby. I'mat the hospital, but I want you to come join me. Baby, please be there. I just need you to come and be with me. I'll send Malik to come and get you," he said.

"Quincy! You can't be serious! After what we went through, you actually want me to do that crazy shit? I mean, she's indirectly the reason why our baby isn't here, remember?"

"Midnight, I know, but she's in distress and the baby might not live. I can't lose another baby. Just be there for me, please, and bypass everything else. I'm begging you. I need you!"

Quincy ended the call and I stood there, astonished, with the phone in my hand. I was puzzled and taken aback by his request. How could he want me to do that dumb shit after what happened? I hung up the phone and realized then that I had Kaelyn on the other line.

"Shit! Hello? Dammit," I said into the receiver, hoping that she was there to talk me out of what would be the biggest decision I had to make in a long time.

"Yeah, yeah, I am here. . . you had me on the phone waiting forever, but I'm here. I figured it was something important. What going on?" Kaelyn asked, inquiring about the last few weeks.

"Long story short, Rachelle is in labor and the baby is in distress. Quincy and I had another argument after having a wonderful night. He wants another baby and I don't know if I can handle him having one with Rachelle. I can't believe this is happening!" I placed my right hand on my head and then touched it to my heart, feeling it palpitate beyond recognition. All of a sudden, the light from the window caught my left hand that held my wedding band, encrusted with diamonds. "For better or for worse," was what my vows stated, and today was another test of our relationship.

"Tamika, what the hell kinda bullshit is this man putting you through? Aren't you kind of tired of dealing with the same thing over and over? He's always placing you in situations where you have to compromise yourself and you are losing!" Kaelyn said, with a hint of anger.

"Kae, I am sorry you feel that way, but this is my life and I have to do what's good for me and mine, just like you do for you and yours," I said, getting tired of being judged for my decisions. They were mine to make.

"Tamika, you are crazy for thinking that man is going to be faithful to you. You are an even bigger fool for thinking he's going to change and love you like you need to be loved. Do you, and don't come crying back to me when he fucks you over raw, yet again!"

The conversation ended right there and I had hot tears streaming down my face out of embarrassment. This is my best friend and she thinks I am a fool. What does everyone else think? I couldn't worry about them right now. I grabbed my phone, keys, and purse and opened the door to leave. I was greeted by Malik, Quincy's best friend.

"He knew you would come through for him. He sent me to come get you," Malik said, eyeballing me up and down.

"Oh, um, okay. . . hey!" I began to wipe my face to mask the sadness I had within me. I lost my child, was losing my husband, and now, I've lost my best friend. I didn't want to talk about it and walked to his truck where he opened the door for me to enter. I placed my seatbelt on and put on my shades to camouflage my red eyes. Malik went around to the driver's side and placed the key in the ignition, but he didn't turn it on. Instead, he looked over at me, waiting for answers that I refused to give to him.

"Are you okay? Why do you look like you were crying?" Malik grabbed my face and looked at me in concern. He was always someone I could depend on to have my back. We had plenty of talks while Quincy and I were having problems during the death of Lanai. He helped me get through, and even allowed me to cry and vent when I needed to.

Malik Wallace was your typical, New York brother. Born and raised in Brooklyn, New York, he was taught the fine art of hustling. I soon learned that he and Quincy did business outside of the city, mostly out of state, like Maryland and Philadelphia, because of the type of work.

When Quincy finally opened up to me about what he does and why so many women have his number, it was told to me that he did party promotions on the side, working with new and up and coming artists, getting them booked. Why he didn't tell me from the beginning, I don't know, but he and Malik partnered up to create *Silver Snake Promotions*. I even went to many of their parties and they networked with a lot of celebrities and musicians. They seemed to be doing well for themselves, and were living the rockstar life, until I came on the scene, demanding answers.

They weren't ready to accept that I was that type of woman that wanted answers about whom her man was with, when, and why. That's how Quincy met Rachelle and they eventually got married a year later. I guess he thought you could turn a hoe into a housewife, but that was almost nine years ago and this is my life we are talking about. Six years into their marriage is when I met Quincy and clearly, nothing has changed. It would only be a matter of time before I became tired of dealing with the same shit. I wasn't about to deal with any more than I already have in this relationship, although it seemed I had reached my maximum.

We promised to keep honest in order to get married, and that was necessary. However, I know that if I knew then, what I know now, we wouldn't have gotten this far. But, I had faith in the relationship.

Unbeknownst to anyone, an attraction developed between Malik and me during the course of our friendship, but we never acted on it. Malik was attractive to everyone and used to play college football before a knee injury sidelined him, so he's far from a dunce. His dark, wavy hair lined up against his head neatly, and his brown eyes resembled milk chocolate kisses.

His caramel skin was rippled with muscles that protruded through his Ed Hardy shirt. His matching jeans hung low on his waist without looking too "ghetto," and landed below his ass. His Timberland boots laced up just enough for him to slide on and off his feet. His hands were manicured and painted clear, and touched my face ever so gently, seeking an answer to his question.

"Tamika, I am not taking you anywhere until you let me know what happened to cause you to cry. Was it Q? I told him he needed to stop his bullshit before he lost you for good. " He pounded his hands together for emphasis.

"Malik, I am okay. I just had an argument with my best friend and that pissed me off. I am so mad I'm being placed in a situation where I have to see his child. I guess the realization of it is setting in," I said, while more tears began to fall.

"Man, Tamika, fuck that! The realization is that Q fucked up and ever since Lala left us, he's been tripping hard, and I keep tellin' him he needs to focus on you and what y'all have. I ain't try'na get all in your business, but you deserve much better and I'm tired of seeing him pull back from you and not give you what you want and need. I think I could…" he stopped short right there, and turned his face to the driver's side window.

"Malik, don't do that. You know you and I have a friendship. I don't like when Q shuts down on me, so why would I allow you to do the same-and you and I have developed a friendship?" I began to cry again, wondering why everyone in my life ends up walking out of my life. Just then, Malik leaned over and kissed my cheeks where my tears stained my face. He kissed my chin and placed his soft lips on mine, his tongue creeping to part mine and begging my mouth to receive his. I was receptive to the affection and we began to kiss in the car, slowly and seductively, as if we both wanted something. We already know what it is and our thoughts were interrupted by my vibrating purse.

"Shit! Hello?" I said, gasping for breath. I looked at Malik who had pangs of guilt written all over his face.

"Tamika, I wanted to know if Malik got there yet. He's not answering his phone and I forgot to tell you that I sent him. "Malik looked at me and put his finger to my lips, telling me to keep quiet about everything. I looked into his eyes and pretended as if nothing happened.

"No, I'm standing outside, waiting for him. He's not here yet, but Kaelyn said there was traffic on the way home so le' me finish talking to her and I'll see you in a bit," I said, as I ended the call and Malik looked at me, wondering what was said.

"Well? What did he say?"

"He wanted to know where you were and if you were with me. Can we just go, please? We've already done something we just may very well regret and I can't block his calls forever," I said, rubbing my hands together with worry.

"A'ight, le' me get you to the hospital before he has a fuckin' fit," Malik said, placing his seatbelt back on.

The ride to Brooklyn was longer than I expected because of the anxiety that I was experiencing, but it brought back a lot of memories. The hospital where Rachelle was having the baby was State University of New York Hospital, and that happened to be the same hospital that I had Lanai in. *How convenient,* I thought to myself, as I watched the GPS in the Ford Expedition that Malik drove. We entered the Jackie Robinson Parkway and, finally, he broke the ice with a simple question.

"Are you as attracted to me as I am to you?" he said, as he cracked the window to the car. It became stuffy all of a sudden and I knew he felt the tension mounting from us, especially when we kissed.

"Malik, are you serious? I can't answer that. I am married to your best friend and, furthermore, I am not in a position to say anything right now. Please don't make this moment any more difficult than it already is. "

I reached into my purse to re-apply my MAC lip-gloss and Malik grabbed my hand, putting pressure on it, and staring at me, gathering thoughts within his head to make a point. "Tamika…we aren't finished yet!" I pulled my hand away and rubbed my wrist, which began to turn red after the force he placed on it.

"Malik, let's just get through the situation at hand. You and I are currently a non-issue. Nothing else matters right now, but this bitch and this child that's about to be born. How the hell am I going to deal with that? He's already got two kids with her, but this brand new baby is the nail in the coffin," I said, getting angrier at the fact that I am with a man that has lied to me on more than one occasion and has children when I haven't a child.

"All the more reason for you to be with a man that has fallen in love with you and wants to give you everything you desire. This is my last time talking about it right now, but later on we will, and then, after that, your decision will change everything. "Malik stared me with steely eyes while we sat at a stop light and said not a word. I knew that things between us would be different, but I didn't have any idea just how much. He reached over and turned on the radio and we sat silently, listening to the radio. I surveyed the area and so much of it became familiar to me. I remembered streets where Quincy and I frequented and I smiled. Brooklyn never lost its flavor and my relationship with Quincy was a strong part of it.

We pulled up in front of the hospital and I gasped as if I lost my breath. Malik went to park the car and would meet me inside later on. I didn't forget what he said to me, but I put that off into the back of my mind. My brain was on maximum overdrive, and I needed to deal with things one thing at a time.

I walked into the sliding doors and announced myself as Tamika Thompson to the nurse asking to see Rachelle Griffin.

"Oh! She's right here. Are you related?" she asked, handing me the visitor's pass.

"Not really," I responded, wanting to hurry up and get upstairs. The nurse at the information desk looked at me strangely and then at the computer monitor. She then instructed me where I needed to go.

"Oh, okay, ma'am. Good luck and thank you for coming to SUNY Hospital for your medical needs. "

The nurse informed me that she's listed under Rachelle Griffin-Thompson.

ON TO THE NEXT ONE

I shook my head and sighed when I found out that the bitch still has his last name, and is still holding on, even though their divorce had been final long ago. Some people just don't know when to move on. I felt like a hypocrite after that thought crossed my mind. Here I am, holding on to a man that has done so much to me, yet I'm still by his side. One day, a lesson will be learned and my gut tells me it will be sooner than later.

"Ma'am, the room for Mrs. Thompson is 342. Please sign your name here to receive a pass. Mr. Thompson is already present," the nurse at the Information desk said, interrupting my thoughts.

I signed my name on the visitor's form and ultimately ended up scratching it out. I wrote Tamika Thompson as a habit but, today, I will be Tamika Adams. I took the guest pass and got into the elevator to go up to the maternity ward. My phone rang as I entered and it was Quincy.

"Hello. I'm in the elevator. I'll see you in a bit," I said, rushing him off the phone. Other people in the elevator looked so happy, but not me. I looked like I needed to commit myself to the loony bin. I was experiencing bouts of anxiety that made me sick inside. Who in their right mind would go to be with their husband while his ex-wife had their baby? Me! That's who! Evil thoughts entered my head; I should have killed the bitch when I had the chance.

I exited the elevator and saw everyone gathered at the window and handing out cigars. Apparently, I was late for the celebration, but I made it, nonetheless.

"Tamika! It's a girl! She's so beautiful! Her name is LaShonda Qiona Griffin-Thompson," he said, hugging me.

"Who named her? Why is her name so close to Lanai? And why does she have your last name?" I asked, in a disgusted tone. My questions were unanswered as, just then, Malik came from the elevator and saw the embrace that Quincy had me in. He shook his head, put on a front, and came to congratulate his best friend.

"Yo, son! Congrats on the new seed! She's a beauty!" Malik said, looking very uncomfortable and attempting to break the tension. He glanced over at me to see my reaction, but I kept my head straight. I was angry and it was overwhelmingly taking over my mind and body.

"Thanks, man! I appreciate it. I want you to be godfather," Quincy said, already making plans to be around. I took this as my cue to go home. My presence wasn't wanted or needed.

"How's Rachelle?" I wanted to know simply for my own well-being and peace of mind that she was okay, because later on, I would kill her for making my life a living hell.

"She's good. Rough delivery, but everything went well and the doctor said…" I cut him off instantly.

"Q, I don't care to know irrelevant details about your ex-wife's delivery when my initial questions were ignored! I, too, have given birth, so I know how it goes down. I'll talk to you later," I said, as I turned and walked away.

Quincy grabbed my arm and I pulled away from him. I had enough of being man-handled for the day and I was going to go home and relax.

"Quincy, don't make a fucking scene. Go be with your new family. This is exactly what she wanted. What kind of a fool do you take me for? She's given you exactly what you always wanted and now Lanai is just a mere memory!"

It was then that Quincy did something I never thought he would ever do.

"Shut the fuck up about Lanai!" he said, with a stinging slap to my face. I was thrown into the waiting room chairs while Malik and others came, restraining him from his violent outburst.

"You son of a bitch! You promised you would never hurt me! I fucking hate you and I want it over! Your shit will be out of my house by tomorrow night. Find someplace else to live!" I yelled and screamed at him while he came to try to rectify his mistake. My busted lip represented the relationship that, in time, would be healed but, never, ever the same. We were too far gone, though. Resentment had taken over and there was no turning back from it.

I walked out of the hospital with my lip bleeding and the left side of my face swelling up fast. I stopped by the sliding doors and dug into my purse to take out my sunglasses. I couldn't go outside like this, but I needed to get out-and fast. I noticed a line of cabs outside, blowing at people to take them home. I had cash on me that would at least take me into the city to take the Metro North, so I raised my hand to flag one down. Just then, I felt a tap on my shoulder and I turned around, startled. It was Malik, coming to see how I was doing.

"I brought you an ice pack for your face. Let me take you back inside so you can be treated. "

"No! I'm fine, Malik. I just want to go home and lay down. I'm very tired and spent from the bullshit that's taken place today. I don't even know why I bothered to come. This was Rachelle getting to me once again. I should have known that as soon as this baby was born, he would forget about Lanai. "

"Tamika, he didn't forget about her. He's just caught up in the moment and needs to come back down to earth. The police want you to press charges against him, but they need a statement from you. Are you going to?"

"No, Malik, I am not pressing charges. I don't want to deal with Quincy anymore, if I can help it. I am done with him and I want to just go. I'm trying to get a cab now.
"

"Let me take you home to get cleaned up, okay?"

I accepted, begrudgingly, and we walked to where he parked his car. I wasn't sure about pressing charges against Quincy for hitting me, but I know he would end up paying for it sooner rather than later. Once Malik dropped me off, I would set the plan in motion. He opened the door for me and I got in, put on my seatbelt, and placed the ice pack on my swollen face that was bruising with every passing minute.

"Jesus! Look at my face! I look like I've been hit with a Mack truck!" I said, viewing the damage to my face in the overhead mirror. As I looked at my face, I saw a dark car suspiciously camped out at the hospital in a parking spot away from others. I could have sworn I saw the same car behind us on the highway but I didn't think anything of it. If it's all starting all over again this time, they would get their intended target, and it wouldn't be me!

I reapplied the pack and sat back while we took a drive. No sooner than I fell asleep, I woke up to Malik touching me lightly. He hadn't taken me home to my house but, instead, took me to his.

"Malik, this isn't the plan. I want to go home to my house in Greenburgh. Please don't play games with me now. I don't have the energy to fight. " I was weary and tired and just wanted things to be normal, but it didn't seem that would ever happen as long as I was living and breathing.

"Tamika, I am not fighting with you. I simply want to finish our talk from earlier and also tend to your face. You don't want the neighbors to see you like this, do you? What would they think?"

He made a valid point, but I couldn't give a damn at this point, about what anyone thought. I was simply tired and bruised after being battered, and wanted to relax.

"Fine, but let's make it quick, please. I could give a shit what the neighbors think. They saw me fight that bitch on my front yard. They know I have 'hood in me," I said, letting out a little chuckle. "Anyway, I have to pack his shit and get it out before tomorrow night. Where he goes, I could give a damn, because he's not going to where he needs to be and that's HELL. "

Malik opened the car door for me and escorted me into his condominium where we were greeted by the doorman. He lived in a quaint little condo in Clinton Hills and it was all his. *He's done well for himself,* I thought, and was secretly proud that he wasn't renting or being another stereotype that society considered 'ghetto'.

He opened the door to his place and we stood in the hallway of his apartment before he escorted me inside. His condo was nice for a bachelor and well-decorated. Dark, purposeful colors with rich burgundy and black accented his living room. The kitchen was grey and white, and the bathroom was an emerald-green. *It was as if every room had a theme*, I thought, as I walked in and observed the scenery.

"My phone. I need to turn it off or else Quincy will think something is wrong," I said, protesting to retrieve it from my purse.

"I think he'll believe something is wrong either way after what happened today. Don't worry about that. Just focus on me taking care of you. I gotchu," he said, placing my purse in the back of his coat closet.

I didn't know how to feel, but this was something that I needed to do. I needed to relax and I took a glance into the mirror in the hallway. Apparently, I needed to take a damned shower and clean up, also. I noticed blood stains on my dress from my bloody lip that I hadn't noticed when I left in haste.

"Malik, can I clean up a bit? Maybe take a shower, please, and wash out my dress, so I can leave and go home. I'm awfully tired. "

"Come with me and I'll turn on the shower for you. Here's my robe!" he said, as he handed me a long, silk, black satin robe. It was somewhat oversized, but it felt very comfortable. He left the room while I changed my clothes and got into the robe. I removed my dress, lace panty, and shoes, placing them in a pile, folded neatly on the bathroom floor. I took a look in the full length mirrorin the bathroom and saw my nipples were curiously erect.

My body was reacting to my suppressed feelings towards Malik. I couldn't wrap my head around it and I don't know what it was, but he made me feel a way I haven't felt in a long time-which was secure. That was Quincy's "job," but he was making it very difficult and this stunt he pulled today fucked it up for him. He and I had been through so much in the last few years, but he never laid a hand on me. The death of Lanai, and him being hurt, put a strain on our relationship; moreso than I was ready to accept.

"There I am making excuses for him again," I said to myself out loud. I brought my hand up to my breasts and noticed my wedding ring. I took it, and my engagement ring, off and placed them in the soap dish above the sink. Just then, Malik walked in to collect my clothes to wash them and saw my silhouette.

"Tamika, are you okay?" Malik said, as his eyes caught my breasts and couldn't remove themselves from them. It was as if he was in a trance.

"I'm fine. I was just getting comfortable and relaxed. I just want to wash up and go home so I can relax and pack up his shit, once again. Can you excuse me so I may wash up and get out of your way?" I said, feeling very uncomfortable at the eyes piercing through me. I felt even more naked than I was supposed to be, and him staring at me wasn't making it any better.

"I'm so sorry, Tamika. Here, let me give you this towel and get out of your way. I'll be out in the living room if you need me," Malik said, before leaving me in the bathroom. I heard the door close behind him and stepped into the standup shower. I pulled the glass doors behind me and was immediately impressed. I needed something like this in our home. The walls began sweating as the hot water pounded against my naked body.

I sat there for a few minutes and washed my face. It began to burn my eyes, especially my lips, but I fought through it. I knew my face was beginning to change colors, but it was something I would have to deal with when I put on makeup. Just then, some soap got into my eye and I forgot I didn't have a towel nearby. I peeked out of the shower to grab the towel left for me off the toilet seat and I saw a shadow standing there. I realized it was Malik watching me while I showered.

"What the fuck? Why are you just standing there?" I closed the door to the shower and cussed him silently. He had some nerve to just be there standing there. Just then, I heard the shower door open and it was Malik.

"You didn't tell me to leave. You just asked what I was doing there," he said, standing there in all his glory. Malik was buck ass naked in front of me and I had nowhere to run.

"Malik, why are you in here? Please don't create a problem we can't come back from," I said, pleading with him to get out. His erection was just staring at me and I knew that it would find its way to me soon.

"We already have a problem. It's Quincy. You think I give a fuck about what he knows anymore? That nigga ain't shit. I didn't even want to be his best man because I knew he was making a big mistake. You are a dime, Tamika. You deserve the best. Now I know I wasn't around, or truly made myself known, but I went from slanging rocks to getting all this on my own, without getting caught up in some bullshit with the law. That, in itself, is a job, but I did it. What I really wanna know is why the fuck am I explaining this shit to you in the shower when all I wanna do is make sweet love to you?"

I gasped at he approached me but, by the time I attempted to protest, his lips already began to touch mine and slowly caressed the injury caused by Quincy's reckless aggression.

"Look at how he fucked up your beautiful face! That nigga is crazy for not taking care of you," he whispered, as he kissed my neck and chin, and began to caress my breasts slowly. He looked at my body that was still in prime condition considering I'd had a child and it showed. My breasts were larger and my hips were wider. He placed his hands on my hips and grabbed my ass, pulling me closer to him. My hair began to get wet and curly as the water splashed on it. I began to protest, but his kisses soon pulled me in. Like sinking in an abyss, my body was pulled in, without any idea of how I was going to be saved. Funny thing is, I think I was already saved from my own personal nightmare.

"Malik, don't!" I said, while grabbing his large shoulders for support.

"Sssshhhhhhh, I haven't even started!" he said, grabbing a sponge and placing soap on it. Malik began to lather up a loofah and began to wash me slowly, caressing every part of my upper body. My shoulders were so tense but the combination of the hot water and the touch of Malik's hand made me feel so much better. I actually began to relax. I placed both hands up against the wall and placed my head down while he washed the back of my neck and traced it slowly down the concave of my back. My lower back responded to his touch, but I jumped when he moved the loofah sponge along my hip.

"Ouch!" I said, as it grazed my hip that was injured when I fell from the blow by Quincy into the hospital chairs. Malik pulled his hand away and bent down to kiss the offended area. His wet lips kissed my hips and he slowly traced his tongue along the outside of my thigh. He grabbed me carefully and turned me around, facing him. I looked down, placing my hand on his shoulder for leverage and he placed my right leg on his left shoulder. He took the sponge, parted my pussy lips and began to wash between my legs, making me tingle in ways I never thought I could. So what if I just had sex with my husband a day ago? This man wanted to be with me and wasn't whoring all over New York.

"Malik, we need to stop," I said half-assed, knowing within my heart that he wouldn't and that, deep down, I didn't want him to. His touches just felt so damned good that, no matter what happened between Quincy and I, it didn't feel as good as Malik's hands. I began to feel his fingers enter me slowly and replace the sponge. He massaged my clit and I began to tingle from the stimulation. I moaned loudly and he placed his other hand in my mouth, causing me to bite his fingers. I tasted myself and I was so sweet on his fingertips. I became more aroused and he responded to it, placing more fingers inside of me and penetrating my walls. I began to buck under pressure as he finger fucked me like he wanted to pop my cherry once more. Harder and harder his hand was inside of me as I threw my head back in the throes of passion. The water beat on my face as I felt myself approaching climax.

He stopped suddenly not wanting my pleasure to end, but to intensify, and stood up.

"You like that feeling? There's more where that came from! Bring that ass over here you sexy bitch!" he said, massaging his ebony dick.

"Yes, boo! I love it!" I felt like I was in a trance and grabbed him by the hand to stand him up in front of me. I leaned in to kiss him and my tongue thrust into his mouth like a snake, waiting for his prey. He grabbed a handful of my hair and turned me around with my ass facing him. I knew what was going to happen next and I was prepared for it. Malik bent me over and pushed his hard, throbbing, chocolate dick into my awaiting slit. I was already wet from the manual stimulation and, coupled with the soapy water, my pussy greeted the penetration.

"Ahhhhhhhhhh," he said, as my tight pussy enveloped him and I felt him throb inside of me. He thrust inside of me with purpose and power and I felt like his spirit was trying to become one with mine.

"Ohhhh…ohhhhhh…damn!" I moaned, enjoying the feeling. My body responded and I began to throw my ass back at him. I already felt myself dripping down my thighs as secretions of both him and I combined making its exit from my canal.

Malik placed his hand on my hips and grabbed a fistful of hair for leverage as he placed his right leg on a ledge in the shower. Harder and harder he pounded into me until I felt like I was losing my balance. I grabbed his wrist behind me and began to yelp loudly as he was bringing me closer and closer to a powerful orgasm. The water began to turn tepid as my internal thermometer began to rise and I felt myself begin to erupt due to the sensual stimulation I was receiving, courtesy of Malik and his Mandingo-sized member.

"Ooooooooooooooh, yeah, babe! Oooh, yeah!" I heard myself say, as I reached the peak of orgasmic bliss and lost total and complete control. The contractions of my pussy on his dick during orgasm triggered his to begin. I felt him throb and drip inside of me and literally grow bigger. Malik banged me harder and harder as if to climb inside of my body.

"Uh…uh…uh…yeah…oh, shit, you sexy bitch! Oh, my God…take all this dick," Malik said, as he emptied his loins inside of me. I felt a gush of warm fluid inside of me and I knew that he came inside of me. My legs lost the feeling in them and I collapsed. Malik stepped out of the shower, grabbed a towel, and wrapped me in it, carrying me to his bedroom. My face was bruised and I looked spent from both the day's events, and also from the erotic whipping that he just unleashed on me.

PLAYING FOR KEEPS

"Tamika! Tamika! Wake up. "

I felt Malik shaking me out of my sleep and I got woozy and instantly aggravated. I wasn't in my own bed and definitely not in my own home. Suddenly, the events of the day replayed in my head and I placed my head in my hands out of frustration.

"Ouch!" I said, obviously not remembering that I was in an extreme amount of pain.

"Your phone has been going off for the last thirty minutes. It's only now that I heard it, because I was asleep, also," Malik said, as he brought me my purse that was hanging on his closet door. I looked around the bedroom and saw clothes all over the floor and towels. I remembered I was in Malik's bedroom and my hair was a mess. Just then, I realized what happened and ran my hands through my hair. I then realized that my wedding rings were missing and I started to ask Malik for them.

"Here you go. I figured you would be looking for them. I'm going to make you some coffee. Your clothes are on the ottoman and you can eat something and then go handle your business. I ordered some food for you and it's in the kitchen. If you need anything, I'll be in my study," Malik said, very professionally. I didn't know how to approach him now.

Our exchange came rushing back to me and I realized just what happened as I slipped on my dress. I would have taken a shower, but I remembered I tried that and no good came from it. I just left well enough alone and checked my text messages, emails, and voicemails. Eight of them were from Quincy, wanting to know where I was, and two were from my mother. My best friend, Kaelyn, also called, but she would have to wait. After her opinion of my relationship, I wasn't eager to butt heads with her again.

"Tamika, are you decent?"

"Hey, Malik, I am. " I had just put on my dress and was putting my shoes on while I listened to the rest of my messages.

"I just wanted to talk to you about what took place between us. " Malik looked at me intensely in the eyes and I began to feel awkward and vulnerable.

"No, please don't. I don't want to discuss this now" I shook my head and began to stand to walk away.

"Tamika, what happened between us was real and it wasn't my intention. Things between us are going to be very different and I don't want you to shun them. Just know that I'm here for you, regardless of what you choose. I know you are going back to that nigga and I can't control your heart. Just know that you control your destiny and this…" He pointed to his chest and waved his hand at the home he made for himself.

"…this is what you will be missing if you walk away from a life with me. Remember that. " With that, he let go of my hand.

"Malik, you've got to understand that what happened was something that took place under stress. "

"Stress, my ass! You wanted me just as much as I wanted you and you didn't put up much of a fucking fight.

"Wow, well, given the circumstances, I can't say that I did, but I don't believe that the decision made was one made with a sound mind. I am still married-and to your best friend. How could we do that to him?"

Everything was coming together now and the reality of it is that I am not any better than Quincy. I did exactly what he did to me, yet worse. Somehow, the evil side of me said that he deserved it after all he did to me.

"Okay, Malik. Let's just keep what happened between us. I will figure out what to do. You know you are my boy, regardless. I just feel like I am no better than him when it comes to what we did. "

"Tamika, the difference is we love each other and you can't deny the feeling. You and I have chemistry that we can't explain. I'm sorry we've held it in for so long, but now is the time we are going to act on it. I'm going to do all I can to make you happy," Malik said, grabbing me to hold me close in his arms. I pulled away from him and walked towards the door.

"Malik, stop! Let's just figure out what we are going to do before we proclaim that we are a couple, which we are not. I need to figure out my situation with Quincy and what to do. We have nothing else left to hold onto," I said, as I began to cry. I was becoming so tired of shedding tears, but that's all I seemed to be doing lately.

"Let me take you home or call for a car to take you home. I know you will choose the latter," Malik said, as he picked up his phone to call a car service.

"Yes, this is 174 Greene Avenue in Clinton Hills. Clinton Terrace. One Female. Five minutes? Okay. Thank you!"

I gathered my things and sat on the side of the bed, waiting for my cab that Malik just called.

"The car service will be here in five minutes. Are you going to be okay?" Malik asked, holding my hand. I pulled it away and adjusted my hair, pulling it in and out of my rubber band, making a new ponytail. I stood up and looked at my Blackberry. I was still receiving messages from Quincy, but now they were text messages. I deleted each one of them as they came in.

"Malik, thank you so much. I'll be fine, so long as I keep my cool and stick to my decision. " I thought to myself how many others times have I kicked him out and he weaseled his way back into my life. I couldn't play the fool anymore. Today was the straw that broke the camel's back. I walked over to the door so Malik could let me out and I could go home. I turned around and kissed him on his cheek. He handed me some dark Tom Ford sunglasses. I smiled and placed them on my face, exiting his building. As I looked to my left, I saw a dark vehicle pull up to the entrance of Malik's house. It looked as if it was my cab from the car service because of the tinted windows, but I was unsure.

"Taxi?" I said, as I tried to peek inside to get the driver's attention. It sped up and drove away. It was then I knew I was in serious trouble yet again. Not only did they see me, but they knew where I was. Whoever it was, saw me leaving Malik's apartment, and that could possibly cause me a load of drama. I decided to cross that bridge when I came to it. Just when I made up my mind, the car service pulled up to take me home.

"28 Teramar Way, Greenburgh, New York. " I gave the driver my address and just sat back as he drove me through Brooklyn, my old stomping ground, and back home to my solace. I had a lot of things to handle and they all pointed back to Quincy.

I was woken up by the ringing of my Blackberry and jumped to answer it.

"Hello," I said, scratching my eyes and waking up, taking a look at my surroundings. I was still on I-95 and about thirty minutes from home, and realized I was in the Bronx, stuck in traffic.

"Tamika," the voice said. It was who I was dreading to speak to for a whole day.

"Yes, Quincy?" I said, voicing my disgust. I didn't want to see him, let alone talk to him, but I knew we would have to come to terms with our relationship, or lack thereof, sooner than later.

"Are you home?" I knew why he wanted to know, but I evaded the question.

"What is it that you want?" I didn't want to play this game anymore and allow him to reach into the deepest crevices of my heart. He knew exactly where to go and how to get there and I locked it off from entry.

"I want to come home and get my things. I spoke to Malik and he told me that you were hurt and bruised."

"Quincy, I don't want to talk about this with you, especially since you are the reason why I am hurt and bruised. Your stuff will be at home, packed up in the living room, at 6pm tomorrow evening. If you don't retrieve it, it'll be donated to charity. It's a wrap for us, sweetie."

"But, what about what we had? You're just going to let that go? Where will I live?"

"Quincy, I don't give a damn where you live. Your things will be at your mother's house. You can live on the street for all I care because love doesn't live here anymore!"

I hung up the phone, tired of hearing his ridiculous whining and looked out the window. My busted lip began to burn and I touched my face. I was crying yet again, over a man that doesn't give a shit about me, or my feelings.

"Ma'am, we are arriving at the destination in approximately ten minutes. Here's your car voucher. Please initial it and keep a copy for yourself," the driver said, as he handed me a slip while we sat at a stop light. I placed my initials on it and waited to go home, to a place that I would soon be leaving for where my heart really was-Brooklyn!

As I exited the vehicle, I realized that things were left exactly as I had when I left a day or so ago. Scents of the candles burning when Quincy and I made love were still faint in the air and I flashbacked to that evening in the bathtub. Little did I know, it would be the very last time he touched me. I hope he treasured every minute because it wouldn't happen again. I went back to when we met and remembered just how caught up I was in him and all the love we made. Just then, my phone rang and on the caller ID, was Kaelyn. I didn't want to talk to her just yet, but I knew she would ring the Blackberry if she didn't hear from me.

"Hello," I said, answering my phone with hesitation.

"Hey, Tamika! How's things with you? Feeling better?" she said, trying to break the ice.

"Hey, girl, I'm okay. Things are not back to normal. As a matter of fact, you don't want to hear this, but it's over for real between me and Q. Rachelle had her baby, and that's why I had to get off the phone with you earlier.

While at the hospital, he and I got into it, and he busted my lip. "

I gave her all the gory details and there was silence on the other line.

"Kae, are you okay over there?" I asked, wondering if she put me on hold or got tired of my rambling and hung up.

"No, I'm here. I just can't believe he put his fucking hands on you and, right now, it's taking everything out of me not to find him and beat the shit out of him, myself. " I could hear the anger in her voice. I'm glad she believed that I was leaving him this time because I was actually sticking to it this time. After all he put me through, if I held on one more time, it would be the death of one of us.

"I'll be okay. Just a bit banged up and Malik tended to me and I'm a little better now. " I failed to mention everything regarding Malik. Anything associated with

Quincy would leave a bad taste in Kaelyn's mouth right now and I didn't want to lose her support when I had just received it again.

"Malik? Hmph! I don't trust none of them fuckers. So, what are you going to do now? Don't get too close to him either. Anyone associated with Quincy is bad business," she said, declaring herself as Quincy's one woman wrecking crew. I knew that she would stand by my side as long as my devotion was to her. That type of alliance was only good when you were doing something pleasing to the other person. If you went another way, they bolted on you and all support was gone.

"I hear you, Kae. Right now, I just wanna get my shit together and move back to Brooklyn. My life was there before him and it will continue to be after him. I have no one but me right now, and I have to move on. Lanai will always be my baby. Nothing can take that from me."

"Okay well if you need me, hit me up. I'll come help you if you want," Kaelyn offered, while I surveyed the house. So much to do and so little time, but it had to be done. I walked into my living room and passed a framed picture of Quincy and me in the hallway, on the way to the kitchen. I looked at it and placed it face down on the table that sat there. He and I are no more and, as much as it pains me, I had to finally come to the realization.

IT'S OVER….

I decided to throw on some clothes and start the process of moving on, and out. I went upstairs and put on some old sweats and a wife beater. I put my hair in a ponytail and put on some music. Hip-hop music always placed me in a good mood and motivated me to keep going. I did just that and started in our bedroom, since that's where the bulk of his things were. I didn't even feel like folding them up. Good thing I kept the boxes from when we moved in a year or so ago, but I didn't think I'd need them so soon.

I gathered the boxes that I needed and took them up to get ready to clean house, literally. With sounds of JayZ's "On To The Next One" blaring throughout my home, I didn't know how much I had accomplished until I began to place back the shoes and realized I had more room in my shoe closet. I would tend to packing my things as soon as I figured out what brownstone I was going to purchase.

I always loved being close to my parents who are up in age and, since I was moving back, I needed to be readily accessible to them and always have that home office I wanted. I didn't forget Trevor's offer to open my own business with the contacts that I've developed. I'd ponder his offer at a later date and work that into where I wanted to live.

I packed all of Quincy's stuff and, after three hours, it was almost 5:30. I was expecting him in thirty minutes to retrieve his items. I went to the garage and got all his odds and ends, like his cameras, golf clubs, and CDs. I gave him the pictures of him and tore up the ones of him and me together. As far as I was concerned, I didn't want him to have any memories of an "us". He placed so much emphasis on making me believe that there was an US when there really wasn't. I believed his lies for the last time and I had dealt with it for the last time.

I picked up a case of records to take out of the garage and was struggling to open the door, when it opened for me. On the other side, was Malik.

"You and I have got to stop meeting like this!" I said, rolling my eyes up in my head.

"What the fuck are you doing in my house?" I said, very bluntly. "I've been prone to surprise visitors before and I wouldn't want to encounter a fresh, dead one on my doorstep! Now, again, what the fuck do you want?" I was beginning to catch an attitude all over again and, coupled with the pain that I was dealing with from earlier, I'd just had enough with the day.

"I came to help Q collect his things. He should be here shortly and said he would meet me here, but I guess I beat him. How are you feeling?" he said to me, as he touched my left cheek and took the boxes from me. All of a sudden, I began to feel a little warm and wished I wasn't so hard on him.

"I'm okay. I just want things over and done with. Time to start over for real," I said, as I fingered my engagement and wedding ring, taking them off and sticking them in my pocket. I'd be returning those to him when he got to the house.

"Okay. Le' me get everything that you can't get out and in the truck, and I'll wait out there for him," Malik said, checking me out in my cleaning gear. My nipples became erect at the sight and notion of them being watched, and I crossed my arms to finish talking to Malik.

"Upstairs, first door on your right is where you will find the bedroom. Right outside, you will see Quincy's things in boxes. I'll be down here with the door open so you can place them in the truck for him. "I wasn't going upstairs for I knew that Quincy was coming soon and I didn't need him to catch me in a compromising position that I couldn't explain.

"A'ight, no problem, Tamika. Thanks. I'ma be done and out of your way in a few," he said, and he went up the stairs to go fetch my soon to be ex-husband's articles.

I opened the door and stuck my head outside. The weather was fabulous considering the way my life was going, but I wasn't going to dwell on the dark cloud that was looming over my head. I was going to do my thing, despite everything. *Maybe if I did things differently from the start, things wouldn't be how they are now*, I surmised.

I thought about how well Quincy and I were supposedly doing, mourning the death of Lanai, and knew that we were both still grieving. As much as I loved him, I would have to let go, but maybe I wasn't giving it a chance. I looked at our wedding picture sitting in a box that I was leaving him and wondered if, maybe, I should just try one more time. *We could always look into counseling,* I thought to myself. We were so happy and he was trying. Just when I thought about taking all his things back, there was someone walking up the driveway.

I wish I had noticed, but I didn't, and I didn't feel too threatened. Malik was bringing stuff from the upstairs and I had already told put the word out to my realtor that, within a month, I'd be moving and wanted it to be as private as possible. This woman was slim, petite, and Hispanic. Despite her size, her posture commanded stature and authority. She had on a dark blazer, white button-down shirt, dark blue jeans, and black Nine West pumps. Her matching Nine West purse was slung over her shoulder. She had on dark sunglasses, which added to her mystery. She kind of reminded me of Rosie Perez or a shorter Jennifer Lopez. Her dark hair framed her face and bounced as she walked towards me. I didn't know what to think but I cautiously listened to every word and watched her every move, just in case I had to haul ass or throw a brick.

"Hello, my name is Jazmine Gonsalez, and I am looking for Quincy. He and I have some unfinished business to tend to. " She removed her sunglasses and I looked in her face to survey her expression. I didn't know why she was here, but I'd have to play it by ear if I wanted some information out of her that would be beneficial to my case. I already knew she was someone that called Q frequently.

"Yes, how can help you? I am his wife," I said, temporarily placing the rings back on my finger and showcasing them to this mystery woman. Clearly, it had no effect because she looked past it and laughed.

"His wife? He never mentioned you. And with reason! You are a fine piece of ass. I'd keep you safe, too, if you were my woman!" she said. I pulled my hand away since she grabbed it, shamelessly flirting. I left that life alone after that incident with Mike and Nic, and wasn't going there again.

"Again, what business is it that you have with Quincy? He'll be here to get his shit, so, either you can wait, or you can tell me what the fuck you want with my husband. " I was losing my patience, especially because she was taking her time and I hated to be left in suspense. Jazmine reached into her pocketbook and took out a business card, smirking as she handed it to me.

"Doesn't look like he'll be your husband for much longer," she said, smirking as she looked at the boxes containing his things outside on the porch. She continued to speak, "Q knows what I want. Make sure he gets this, please, so he knows I was here. Enjoy your day, Tamika!"she said, as she laughed and walked away. I glanced at the business card and noticed a whiff of perfume. I also flipped it over and saw a lipstick kiss on it. *How original,* I thought, and flipped it back over. I saw her name and her phone number, as well as her tag line- *WHATEVER YOU WANT, I GOT IT.*

Apparently, whatever she had, Quincy wanted or had and, either way, he could keep it, because I wasn't engaging in any competition. Thoughts of reconciliation disappeared as soon as she arrived, which lead me to think that I finally recognized the red flags that put the sense back into me.

Just as I turned around to go back into the house, I heard a car drive by. Assuming it was the woman, Jazmine, that just left, I walked closer to the sidewalk. The dark car slowed down close to me, the window opened slightly, and a black-gloved hand dropped a red rose at my feet. I jumped back and it veered off, leaving tire marks in the middle of the street. I screamed in fright and Malik came rushing to my aid. Just then, Quincy turned the corner and pulled into our driveway. I knew then that my decision to leave him was solid. It was literally becoming a matter of life and death!

"What the hell? Tamika, who was that?" Quincy asked, as I held the thorny, red rose in my hand. He looked at me, waiting for an answer, and I looked at him, waiting for one myself. I began to tear up and I just shook my head.

"Quincy, it's starting yet again or, shall I say, it never ended. So long as I am with you, I will never be happy. Here's your rose and here's a message for you," I said, as I handed him the business card that Jazmine left for him. He looked at it, puzzled, and turned it over to see the message she left for him in the form of a kiss.

"Tamika, it's not what you think. That's not what this means!" Quincy said, pleading his case. It didn't matter to me anymore because I knew that it was over for us and this time, I was determined to stick to it, not like the other times.

"Q, I don't want to hear it. It's never what it seems and I'm sick and tired of trying to figure out what to do. I love you enough to let you go and I wish you would do the same for me," I said, as I turned and began to walk away. This would be the last time I walked away from him and, if I could stand it, I wouldn't go back. Little did I know that once again our paths would end up crossing and it would be sooner rather than later.

A few weeks passed and Quincy came to retrieve his belongings. He, of course, tried to convince me that what happened was something I could forgive. I don't care what he did in the past. The most disrespectful thing he could have done was to put his hands on me. I was tired of thinking about Quincy, and decided to straighten up and put some clothes away, then take a ride to the beach. It was almost Memorial Day weekend and the weather was relatively warm. I loved this time of year because it reminded me of times with Lanai, and how much fun we would have.

I grabbed the vacuum and began to remove some of the clutter and mess that was left behind from Quincy. Somehow, the house looked so much more spacious without him or his belongings here. It was a blessing and a curse, especially since we came to Greenburgh with the mindset to get rid of the drama in our lives, yet it's the same drama that has caused me to want to sell the home. I'd begun to speak to the realtor and, as luck would have it, I would be able to move within the next three months, which brought me a lot of happiness. It's the small things that bring me the most joy now.

I dusted what was necessary and put my vacuum away with time to spare. Thoughts of me going back to work ran through my mind. I wasn't ready to go back to corporate America, but with Quincy out of my life and me selling the home, I would be the sole provider for myself once more. I guess I would adapt a personality like those women on the HBO show, "Sex and the City". My guess is I would be more like Miranda, the workaholic lawyer that was very pessimistic regarding love. After all that I've been through, I think that character is ideal for me. Just then, my house phone, which never rings, jolted me out of my thoughts.

"Hello," I said, expressing joy on my end. I was content with how my life would be, now that it's finally moving in a positive direction.

"Hey, Tamika!" the caller said, sounding apprehensive. I knew right away who it was and my heart skipped five heartbeats. I began to stammer and lost my train of thought immediately. I didn't know he'd have this effect on me. I gathered my thoughts quickly and tried to maintain the composure I had lost at the sound of his voice.

"Malik! I didn't expect you to call me on the home phone, ever. How have you been? It's been a few weeks since I've seen you," I said, trying to sound as casual as possible. I had been waiting for his call, however, I never initiated calling him. I didn't want to make something out of nothing.

"I wasn't sure if you wanted to hear from me, but I took a chance to call and see if you not only wanted to see me, but if you wanted to go out to dinner. I'll come get you and bring you back to the city," he said, sounding like a child that just unwrapped his new toy. I was skeptical, but I decided not to waste the day-and I was going out, anyway.

"Malik, I was going to the beach today. You are more than welcome to join me if you choose, but I wanted to spend some time alone and just relax. I hope you don't mind. Your offer for dinner sounds tempting, especially since I haven't cooked in weeks. "I looked over at the empty sink and at my fridge that had nothing but frozen foods and water. I had all intentions on doing some grocery shopping, but all I had been doing is eating, cleaning, and sleeping.

"Here's what I'll do! I'll meet you at the beach and we'll talk and hang out, and then we'll come back to my place and go out to dinner. I really want to see you and it's not about sex. I miss my friend, Tamika. Quincy's been talking about you every day and I cannot resist thinking evil thoughts about what he did to you, and how I want to be that man in your life. You know what? Let's finish this in about two hours, and then we can go from there. "

I thought to myself that I needed to eat because those frozen foods that I've had are making me sick. It might be because its artificial. I also wanted some time for me but I do enjoy Malik's company. I looked in my closet while on the phone with him and decided quickly on a red maxi dress and some strappy gladiator sandals. I packed them in a bag, along with my essentials, and got dressed to go to the beach. As much as I loved it up here, there was nothing like going to one of my favorite beaches, Orchard Beach.

"Okay, Malik. You sold me on dinner, and I'm sorry I disappeared. I just needed some time for myself to get my mind right. We'll talk soon when I am done with the beach. I'm going to Orchard Beach in the Bronx. "

We ended our call and I grabbed my Blackberry and the charger. I had nine text messages that I refused to check. I already know they were Quincy, texting me to say "hello". He's been doing that for the last few weeks, and I used to answer, but, then he used to overextend it and make me feel guilty about kicking him out and leaving him. My parents say I should try to work it out with him, but I refuse to be a beating stick for any man, mentally or physically, anymore.

Quincy was the last straw after a string of bad decisions regarding men, dating back to college. My mother was a strong advocate for letting "bygones be bygones," even if it meant dealing with shit that you had no business putting up with. My dad and she were married for forty-seven years, and they went through so much ,including adultery, physical and mental abuse, and sickness, but stuck it out because of the vows they took. Maybe that's why tolerated so much when I didn't. I didn't want to end up like my parents, being in an unhappy marriage. There's a difference between being "happily married" and simply "married".

Now, don't get me wrong-I always loved Quincy and believe in trying, but when it comes to a point when the end doesn't justify the means, and I am wasting my time, then it's time to go. I married Quincy under the false pretense that things would change between us, but they got worse and I went nowhere but down since then. I needed my life back again.

I was tired of starting over and over again in my head, but not really doing it. I've already dealt with trying with Trevor and a lot of good that did. I sighed and checked the house, turned on the alarm system, and left to go relax for a while, basking in the eighty-degree weather. May was turning out to be a fabulous month. It was then that I looked at the calendar and saw that our anniversary was approaching.

I had been dealing with Quincy for over three years and I could chronicle all the bullshit he put me through in a book. Maybe, one day, I'd go ahead and write a book and tell the world what I had encountered with a man who I thought loved me. But, for now, my thoughts remained my own.

I arrived at the beach, removed my towel and portable radio, and grabbed my beach bag. The things I needed for dinner with Malik remained in my car for I would get ready later on. I wanted this day to be peaceful and relaxing. I set up shop on a small corner of the beach where there were children playing. I, of course, thought of my daughter and decided to go take a dip for old time's sake. The water was nice and tepid, considering it wasn't super-hot outside. My black bikini showed off all my curves and fit me more snugly than last summer. My curves stood out even more so after having Lanai, and all the men were like sharks. If I wanted to snag a man, today would be the perfect day.

I ventured to the water and took a swim out to the buoy floating in the water, but the lifeguard called me back for fear of trouble. He wasn't even on duty, but I guess the fear of a drowning victim while off duty scared him. I had enough and obliged his request, returning to my towel and laying down to dry off and maybe get a nap. The sun always feels better after coming out of the water. I slathered on some suntan lotion and replaced my sunglasses to protect my eyes. I lay down and soon drifted off to sleep, waking up to my Blackberry ringing.

"He-hello," I said, groggily. I didn't think I was asleep that long, but my mouth felt dry as hell and I felt dizzy.

"Quincy?" I said, trying to regain my focus.

"It's Malik. " He sounded irritated and I think I messed up big-time, thinking he was someone else.

"I'm sorry, Malik! I just woke up and I am so discombobulated. Where are you?"I said, sitting up on the towel and gathering my things.

"Tamika, I see you. I am walking towards you right now. " Just then, I turned around to see the dark figure walking towards me until his shape blocked out the sun's rays from my eyes. I looked up at him and smiled. He stretched out his hand for me to grab and hauled me up. I was practically catapulted into the air by him, and his hand hit my breast, moving my bikini top to the side.

"Oh, shit! I'm sorry, Tamika! Here, let me get the towel. " I looked down at my top and caught a glimpse of his footwear.

This man had on wheat Timberlands in eighty-degree weather. I burst out laughing and couldn't control myself after that. All nervousness went out the window and I realized why I loved hanging out with him so much; he's freaking hilarious in the things he does, and it's not even on purpose.

"Aye, what's so damn funny?" Malik asked, clearly annoyed with my outbursts of laughter, but who wears boots to the beach?

"Tamika, I am not a beach dude and I never was that dude. I just came because I wanted to spend time with you and take you out. Had I wanted to come to the beach, I'd have joined you, especially since I received an invite. "

Malik looked like he was getting an attitude and I was making him feel uncomfortable. I grabbed his hand and looked at him, smiling.

"Let's go eat something!" I said, gathering my things. He bent down and picked up the rest of my things while I wrapped myself in my towel. I saw him eyeing my ass from my peripheral vision and I knew it was going to be a long night.

STARTING OVER, YET AGAIN...

By the time we got to Brooklyn, I was absolutely starving. Malik had to pull over to a store and get me a bottle of ginger ale. I would have gotten something to eat before I went to the beach, but I was taught not to swim soon after eating for fear of getting a cramp. Now, I was experiencing what felt likegas pains like you would never imagine. I always loved traveling back to the city when I could, and driving back made me happy that I was making my plans to relocate. Just then, Malik called and stirred my thoughts.

"Tamika, we're gonna park your car in the garage and take my car so we don't use up any unnecessary gas. You can change upstairs and we can be on the way. Our reservations are at six pm at the Sugar Bar," Malik said, sounding very excited. I could tell he was the type of man that loved doing things for his woman. I wondered what it would be like for us as a couple, but it's taboo to date your ex's friend. My momma always said, "one man's trash is another man's treasure," and Malik was, indeed, treating me like a diamond that he's brushed off and keeping for himself.

I parked my car in the garage as he advised and he greeted me at the building door. He allowed me to use his parking spot and the attendant was pleased to see me. It made me wonder what was said about me, and who he wanted me to be. We walked up to the lobby and he opened the door for me, placing his hand around my waist to guide me inside. He pressed the elevator door and allowed me to enter first. I could tell he wanted to say something but wasn't sure of what.

"Thank you in advance for spending the day with me. It was very nice of you to think of me, despite your busy schedule. "

"It is simply my pleasure. It's a welcome distraction with all that's taken place the last few months. The thought of it makes me sick, actually, but being around you causes me to forget the negative things and actually remember to laugh, and that's something I haven't done in a lil' while. "

"Well, Tamika, that's what I was trying to do today and I am happy that my mission has been accomplished and we haven't even done all that I want to do for you. Let's get you ready for the evening's events, and you can be the judge," he said, as we exited the elevator. I had no idea what the evening would consist of, but it seemed as if this was turning into a real date with my husband's best friend. Was my evening doomed before it even began?

I began to get a nervous feeling in my stomach, even before we entered the apartment, but I don't know if it was hunger or guilt. I decided that it was nerves and starvation and drank some more of the ginger ale that Malik bought me on the way to his house. I grabbed my bag and went into the bathroom to get ready for the evening. All of a sudden, I felt like I needed to throw up and ran towards the toilet and hurled nothing but air and liquid. I didn't think anything of it until I realized that I hadn't had my period in about two months.

I grabbed my purse and opened my calendar to the months of April and May. My last period was in the early part of March and nothing followed. I saton the toilet seat, trying to see how this could happen and realized I had sex with both Quincy and Malik within days of each other. I began to breathe heavily and attempted to catch my breath, but it was too late. I got off the toilet and soon collapsed on the bathroom floor.

"Tamika! Are you okay?" I vaguely heard Malik say, as he pounded on the bathroom door feverishly to check on me. He used his forearm to push the door open, breaking the lock and finding me on the bathroom floor.

"Oh,my God! Tamika, are you okay? Talk to me!" he said, trying to shake me into consciousness. I was fading fast and he turned on the bathroom sink and grabbed some cold water in a cup to give me to drink. As soon as the cup hit my lips, I started to vomit some more. Malik picked me up, held my hair, and hoisted me over the toilet seat to finish releasing whatever was within my body. Sadly, it was nothing but bile and water.

"I'm so sorry, Malik! I, I..." I began to bring some more water up, while dry heaving and I felt faint. I guess I wasn't going to go out tonight, but him and I had to talk because this was a problem that wasn't going to go away for more reasons than I could count.

Malik picked me up by the arm and led me to the living room to have a seat. He sat down next to me and began to interrogate me about what could possibly wrong. I would have this conversation once again with my soon to be ex-husband and I know, depending on who that is, it could turn out very badly.

"Tamika, is there something you need to tell me?" Malik asked. He already knew the answer but wanted to hear it directly from me.

"Malik, I think I'm pregnant. "

Malik exhaled as if he was holding his breath forever. I continued explaining how I was feeling and how it would affect our budding relationship if there were to be one.

"The problem with this pregnancy, if there is indeed one, is that I don't know if it's yours or Quincy's," I said, beginning to cry. The realization of me having a bastard child was emotionally draining and I didn't want to be one of those trifling bitches on the Maury Povich show that didn't know who the father was.

"Tamika, who's baby do you want it to be?" Malik said, being very serious.

"Malik,it's not about whose baby it is, really. It's about the fact that I'm having an affair with my husband's best friend and may be pregnant by him. It is not an ideal situation. "

"I know, Tamika, but it's what we have to deal with. I love you enough to deal with whatever happens. There's a fifty-percent chance that's it is my baby, I know, but I love you enough to be with you, regardless, and raise it as my own. I want to make you my wife, and Q and I ain't been right since he moved out. There's a lot that's going on, but it's not time to let you in on it. "

I was becoming tired of the lies and secrets and I was getting nauseous at the idea of being caught up in more drama. I needed to know what was going on before I made a decision because, somehow, things always come back to me and affect me adversely.

"Malik, if you are going to lie to me, then I'm leaving. I don't need to deal with this bullshit anymore. I left a relationship because of drama and I'm not beginning one with you based around it. It's bad enough we started this relationship the way we did. Do I regret it? No, but I need to know what's going on!"

I was borderline whining now, trying to have him tell me the truth about how he was feeling. I hated sounding like a whiny female but, lately, I've been every stereotype that I had previously detested.

"Tamika, if you trust me and love me as much as I love you, you will wait for me to tell you what's going on. Let's just rest tonight and I'll have the restaurant deliver to us. I know the manager and he'll do me that, solid. No biggie," Malik said, while picking up the phone to call the restaurant. We were sitting down and pondering what we were going to do.

My head was throbbing as I sat on the couch, just thinking about where my life would be had I not met Quincy. I would be single, successful, and still living in New York, with no problems… I damned sure wouldn't be on my way to being divorced, and I wouldn't be cheating with Malik. But, that means I wouldn't be pregnant and in love, with someone who loves me just as much.

Just as I thought to take a nap, my phone rang and it was my mother. What a fine time for her to call and invade my mind. As much as I loved my mother, she had a way of making my decision, any decision I made, a horrible one, even though it was what I chose to do. I picked up my phone on the fourth ring, right before it went to voicemail, and was greeted by my mother's singsong voice.

"Hello, Mother!" I said, anticipating a long, drawn out conversation about nothing.

"Tamika, where have you been? Your father and I have been worried sick about you! Your brother, Calvin, called me and told me you were selling the house and moving back home. Why do I have to hear it from someone else?" I knew she would confront me about leaving Quincy, but her focus was now the house since he bought it for Lanai and I to live in.

"Ma, I had to leave Quincy! He cheated on me, lead a double life, almost got me killed, and now he put his hands on me. How much more, seriously, was I supposed to take? And when did Calvin come home? He can keep you updated about me and he just came out the military? How come he never called me or came by? You know, what I don't want to know about him. He's not helping my situation at all. "

"So, shacking up with Quincy's best friend helps the situation? I saw how Malik looked at you when you were at the hospital, and at La's funeral. I wear glasses, but I know lust and attraction. That man wants you to himself and he's going to do whatever to help himself to Quincy's leftovers."

My mother was keen to everything but the right thing. She always wanted to be right, even when she knew it wouldn't make us happy. Her way was the right way and that's why, when her and daddy fought, we stayed out of it because we knew, sooner or later, he would hit her, leave, come back, and they would be just fine. I was the oldest and experienced most of the violence in the family. I had to protect my brother from the fuckery, but it was too late it seemed. He was sucked in and now calls our mother to tell her everything that goes on in my life. I made a note to myself to call Calvin and tell him that some things are to be with me and me only.

"Mother, my marriage, or lack thereof, is irreparable and, quite frankly, none of your business. The only thing you should be worried or concerned about is my happiness. You haven't even asked if I was okay. All you care about is Quincy! Do you even care he put his hands on me?"

Then my mother said something I never, ever thought she would say to me.

"Well, Tamika, what did you say to make him hit you?"

I held the phone away from my ear in astonishment. I couldn't believe what I heard. My mother really justified Quincy hitting me because of something I may have said. *How could she have said something like that?* I thought, then I remembered that Daddy used to knock her around occasionally and she was taught to deal with it, because he was paying the bills and providing for my brother and me.

"Momma, you didn't say that! Tell me you didn't. You know what? I am so damned happy that I left home when I did, because I would live my life in fear of you and everyone else. Matter of fact, a lot of good that did because it's yours and daddy's fault why I have such a fucked up outlook on life, love, and men! Thanks for nothing!" I yelled, hanging up the phone.

"What's all the yellin' about? Tamika, are you okay?" Malik came into the living room from his bedroom, holding a glass of wine in his hand. I couldn't answer him and began to sob into my hands. My face was covered with tears and my eyes became instantly red.

"My mother just upset me Malik with her phone call. She said it was my fault that Quincy hit me and I shouldn't leave him. I should stick around and deal with it for the sake of our marriage. She also mentioned that she knows that you want to take me from him," I said. Even through the tears, I felt myself blushing at the admission of his desire for me.

"Tamika, Quincy has proven time and time again that he doesn't want to be around you, nor be with you as his wife. He's cheated on you numerous occasions and physically and emotionally abused you. Your mother has some issues and I think you might want to move on from your family. They tend to pull you down. Now, I can be your family if you want, and love you unconditionally as I much as you will allow, but you have to let me."

I looked into Malik's light brown eyes and all I saw was sincerity and genuine love. I wasn't sure how I was going to handle it, but I knew that things would have to be better than they were before. Malik leaned over and kissed me as he got up to answer the door. I took off my shoes and cuddled up on the couch, grabbing the throw and the remote. This was going to be our first night as a couple.

"Malik, yes, I want you to love me and, as much drama as I've been through, your love is a welcome distraction and gives me some normalcy. For that, I thank you!" He placed the food in the kitchen, served a plate for me, and began slowly feeding me my dinner. My stomach was rumbling due to hunger and because of nerves. I decided I would have this baby, not for anyone else, but for myself. The only thing that was worrying me is if it was Quincy's baby, what would I do?

Bound By Lies

<u>A LOVE LIKE THIS</u>

My first night with Malik was very different, even though we were supposed to go out. We never ended up going out to dinner and, with the interruption of the argument with my mother and my possible pregnancy with Quincy, I had a lot of shit on my brain, so, it was very restless. Malik held me close and made sure I was okay. I was nauseous on several occasions and he stayed up with me until I was comfortable to fall back asleep.

"So, what are we going to do?" Malik said, stroking my hair while my head lay on his shoulder. It felt so comforting being in his nook, but it took everything in my power not to worry about what would happen. I couldn't sleep and shifted frequently in his arms the night before.

"I'm going to get an appointment with the doctor and then try to figure out whose baby this is, so I can live my life accordingly..." I said, with thoughts of my future as a single mother.

Malik arose abruptly and turned to look directly in my eyes. He was angry as hell, but not enough for me to be scared of him. I had enough of abusive relationships and I wasn't going to deal with it from him also. I looked at him and listened intently as he spoke with a raised voice.

"Tamika, are you going to let me in or what? I said I would be there for you, and here the fuck you are planning for a future with Quincy or alone. I told you I loved you and wanted to be with you! I think you are secretly praying that this baby is his! He don't fucking want you! I want you!" Malik said, yelling and clenching his fist. He got up and walked away, leaving me stunned. I didn't realize that he felt that way and I sure as hell didn't know that's how I was coming off.

"Malik, I know you love me and always have, but I have to look out for me. I'm tired of people claiming they have my back and then walking away when it gets too heavy for them. Quincy..." I was interrupted as soon as the words left my lips.

"I am sick and fucking tired of hearing about that nigga! Here's what you do! Figure your shit out and if you love me or not, and let me know if that's my baby! If it is, then let me know and I'll take care of him/her. If it's Quincy's, then I wish you both a long, miserable life together because you both deserve each other. I'm out...you know how to exit!"

Malik walked into his bedroom and shut the door. I, for one, was shocked that he reacted like that, but, in a sense, I expected it. I made it so and I had to make a decision to deal with this on my own. Time to move forward and to live for this life I had because, as of right now, it was all I had left. I grabbed my things, got ready to leave, and thought of what Malik said. I did fall in love with him, but my obligation was to my husband and our child.

As I stepped out of the elevator, my phone rang and it was Quincy. Against my better judgment, I answered it and wasn't surprised at what I heard.

"Hey, Tamika!" he said, sounding so sexy, but I knew of his violent ways. I hadn't heard from him in a while, after he moved his things out of the house. I was still waiting for a call back from my realtor, but I wasn't going to wait. With what Malik told me, I knew I had to move back to New York,get my business up and running, and care for myself. I was more important than anyone else at this point.

"Hello, Quincy. I guess all has been well for you and your family!" I said, as coldly as possible, referring to his children with Rachelle. I still held a grudge and wanted him to know it. He was the reason for the loss of our child and I wanted him to remember it every chance he got.

"The baby is fine, Midnight, but I miss…" I stopped him right there.

"Quincy, please don't call me that anymore because I amnot that. I am just your soon to be ex-wife and the bitch you've turned me into. Please,let's make this as painless as possible. "I hated talking to him about frivolous things, especially when we were at odds.

"Well, I wanted to talk to you about us. I wanted to know if you were pregnant. "

Silence was all that was heard, until an echo was heard in my throat when I gulped. I could have sworn he heard it and I didn't know how to respond.

"Tamika, are you there? We really need to talk. Are you at work? I wanted to meet you so we could discuss some matters, and that was one of them that popped up. I'm in the city right now and I can meet you briefly, if possible. "

"Meet me at the corner of 33rd and 7th Avenue by the Gap Store in thirty minutes. I'll be there and we can speak briefly before I go on about my day!"

I ended the call and felt the butterflies began to erupt in my stomach. How the hell did he know that I was pregnant? He did the same when I was pregnant with Lanai! The more I felt anxious,the more the butterflies jumbled around in my tummy, and I knew it wasn't for the fact that I wasn't that far along, yet, or I'd have thought that the baby was moving, but while I had my mind on it, I called the doctor to make an appointment.

"Doctor's office!" the receptionist said, as she answered the phone.

"Yes, my name is Tamika Thompson and I'd like to make an appointment. I believe I am pregnant. " Just saying that made me take a long breath as if I was holding it in forever. She proceeded to take all my information and it would be in a few days. I set the appointment in my Blackberry, with a reminder, and began the drive to 34th Street.

After being in the suburbs for so long, I looked forward to the excitement of the city and what it means. It didn't take long to cross the Manhattan Bridge and I arrived sooner than I thought. I parked the car in a garage near the Empire State Building and walked over to our designated meeting place. As soon as I arrived, I received a call from Quincy and instantly got annoyed.

"Yes! I don't see you! Where are you?" I said, wanting to get this over with very quickly.

"Can you come over to the hotel where I've been staying? I know its short notice, but I wanted to see you privately, without too many people around. Please, Tamika!"

"I wasn't in the mood to be around you like that after what's been going on. You asked a question and I just wanted to give your answer which could have been over with by answering you on the phone. " I was getting more agitated at the thought of seeing him, but this would prove to Malik that I wasn't in love with Quincy anymore, and I wanted to be with him. I was willing to do whatever I needed to prove to Malik that our love was real and it wasn't a rebound thing.

"Please, Tamika, I want to give you some things and they are personal.

"He was pleading his case something terrible and I was getting nauseous again at what he had to give me, but the back and forth was tiring me out.

"Fine! Just tell me where the fuck you want me to meet you so we can get this shit over with. I'm tired of you making me bend over backwards for you when you don't do the same for me!"

Quincy told me he had moved out of his mother's house months ago because she couldn't take him leaving for long periods of time and then coming back at all hours of the night. No matter how old you seem to be, your parents always see you as a child, and he was a grown ass man as he saw it. He had since moved into a condo in the city to give him access to his kids with Rachelle, as well as business in New Jersey. He and Malik are in talks secretly to disband their business and operate under separate entities, but I'm not supposed to know.

As I walked over to the hotel, I was impressed with the style of the décor, which didn't surprise me too much because Quincy always liked to have the finer things, and it showed in his wardrobe as well as his living situation. Our home was a mini mansion when we purchased it, and it was decorated mostly by Q, who had a knack for paying attention to detail. A shame it wasn't applied to his constant lying and cheating. I entered the elevator and pressed twenty-eight to go upstairs to end this once and for all.

PANDORA'S BOX

I took a deep breath when the elevator doors opened and I felt that feeling in my stomach all over again. As I walked, the click-clack of my heels against the linoleum was the only thing that was heard. I observed the beige wallpaper and the lights in the hallway. There was a mirror under one and I fixed my hair and makeup briefly to make sure I looked nothing less than perfect. No, I didn't love him anymore, but I couldn't help but want to look like I had moved on from him and was happy, even though inside, I was falling apart at the prospect of seeing him. It had been a few months and we only corresponded via phone and text message. I rang the bell on the door and held my breath for him to respond.

"Tamika! You made it! I was afraid you wouldn't come like you said," he said, embracing me tightly and giving me a kiss on my forehead. I hated when he did that but he's a creature of habit. I stiffened up and he noticed my change in response to him.

"Hello, Quincy! How are you? You look good, as usual!" I said, as dryly as possible. The truth was he was looking mighty tasty and I wanted to run into his arms out of habit, but I couldn't, because he hurt me so much in the past that my heart wouldn't let it go. The healing wasn't complete yet because there were so many other aspects that he affected unknowingly, and my trust was one of them.

"Midnight, you are glowing! You look so damned good. How's everything? Did the house sell yet? The lawyer called me the other day, asking me to sign off my rights to it since we are still married and you are selling it solely under your name."

"Let's cut the small talk," I said, taking my purse off and sitting down on the edge of the bed.

"And, furthermore, please don't call me Midnight; she's dead and gone. I don't know where you have that bitch buried, but she doesn't reside within me anymore. " I rolled my eyes and crossed my legs, with my stilettos dangling off my toes. My feet were a little sore because of the walk when I intended on driving, but I was glad to relax, even if I was slightly uncomfortable as to where. The silence became deafening, knowing we had to hash some things out, so I broke the tension and asked questions that I wanted answers to.

"Quincy, what do you have to give me?"

"I have a lot of things to give you, Tamika. First off, I wanted to apologize for all the things that transpired, and being alone gave me the time I needed to realize that I just thought so selfishly and only of myself. I wanted you and her;you were always, and have been my heart. I felt like I died the moment that I thought I would lose you forever and, as luck would have it, I did. "

He said all I needed to hear, and then some, but wasn't finished by a long shot. My throat began to burn from holding in the tears and I instantly began to tremble and shake. He disappeared and went to the kitchen, emerging shortly with a glass of water and some tissue. Apparently, he had more to say and wasn't going to end with just that.

"Thank you," I said, as I wiped my face and took a sip of water. I had a lot of questions and today would be the day that they would be answered. I got up, placing my water glass on his side table and walked over to the living room mantelpiece, where I saw a picture frame of Quincy and myself on our wedding day. I remember that day so vividly and knowing what he had done to me, I still went through with it. My parents were disappointed in me but, for the sake of my happiness, they put up a hell of a front.

I fingered it slowly as more tears fell unto the glass. As if possessed, I held it above my head and threw it furiously onto his hardwood floor, breaking it into a hundred pieces. It was as if I broke his heart as he had broken mine so many times in so many years! Glass shattered everywhere as I broke the picture of us that used to be displayed on the mantelpiece.

"I loved you! I trusted you!" I yelled, as I realized that love had nothing to do with it. This was pure, unadulterated greed. I'm the bitch that gave him money when he needed it and the one he called when he needed to cum. I bent down slowly, hovering over the shattered pieces of glass that represented four years of lies, deceit, and betrayal.

It was then that I realized our relationship was nothing more than a charade. I was a pawn in his sick and twisted game. I slowly grabbed the glass within my hands, causing the shards to puncture my fingertips.

"Tamika, NO! Don't do that, baby!"

"Fuck you, Quincy!" I retorted in disgust, as I pulled away from his grasp.

"Look at what the fuck you made me do!" I said, as I watched my hands bleed slowly and my heartbeat accelerated with anger. I couldn't breathe and felt like I was having an anxiety attack.

With all that I've been through, I'd not be surprised if I did. I'd been prone to them recently with all of the drama that was brought my way. The last thirty days resonated in my head as the straw that broke the camel's back. Four years of bullshit and this relationship is what stuck in my head as the worst part of my life. I began to feel faint as unconsciousness set in. I don't know if I was dying, but anything was better than dealing with Quincy and his shitload of lies.

Never did I believe that our lives would be disrupted in such a manner. If I knew then, what I know now, my life would be so different!

"What the hell is wrong with you, Tamika? How are you going to just come in my home and destroy it? I thought we weren't going to do this. Damn, Tamika!"

"Quincy, you say the same thing every single fucking time. You apologize and then you do the same thing over and over again. I'm tired of taking you and your lying ass back! The final straw was at the hospital. How could you do that to me? I was your everything and you were mine. I trusted you and, even after you go and get that bitch pregnant, I marry you! What kind of fucking fool am I?"

"You dumb bitch! I'd not have slept with anyone else if you didn't push me to it. You nag too got-dayum much! I can never say, nor do, anything right. You are always the perfect one!" Quincy knelt down beside me, unsure of whether he should kiss me or knock me the hell out.

In my daze, I noticed him grabbing his head in confusion. Glass everywhere caused shards to embed themselves into his hands as he tried to lift me up off the floor. I slapped his hand away in anger.

"If you really fucking cared about me, you'd not have put me through this bullshit! We weren't always like this, Quincy!" I slurred my words as my fingers ached with the pain of loving him, as well as the glass lying on the floor beneath me. He looked at me with tears in his eyes. He knows the truth just like I do and I'm wishing he wanted things to change just as much as I do. Will they change?

"Quincy, you almost had me killed! I was almost bludgeoned to death by Rachelle! You had some bitch, who I had no idea about, coming to kill me for your trifling ass and you don't even give a damn. You knew exactly who was stalking me and sending me all those bullshit roses!" I grabbed his hands and pulled them off of me.

Quincy gazed into my eyes and looked as if he wanted to cry. He was finally seeing the pain that he's been causing me.

"Tamika, I've never been one to be in a relationship without letting go of others that may have interest. It's all been so new to me," Quincy explained.

I rolled my eyes at his lame attempt at an excuse for his behavior.

"You can't be serious with this lame ass excuse! You kept me as a fallback bitch? Is that what it was? Q, you know I would've gone to the ends of the earth for you and back. All you had to do was tell me the truth-that we were not exclusive as it was assumed, instead of me looking and feeling like an ass. I was defending you against my family and friends, all the while watching you be with countless women under my nose. How unfair is that?" I was getting frustrated and sat up from his lap and walked over to the window.

The sun was setting and tears started to fall from my face again. My fingers ached from the glass and my throat felt like it was on fire from screaming. The more I thought about what he did, the more I didn't regret what I eventually ended up doing.

"Don't fucking touch me you piece of shit! You lied too many fucking times for me to ever trust you again! I hate you! I hate you! The things I could have done to get you back and, because I loved you, I didn't. I slept with my friend and her husband! I could have been a lesbian and it wouldn't have mattered. You were still a whore!"

Quincy's face dropped and he couldn't believe all I said. The truth was really coming out today and he didn't expect that blow to his ego.

"What the fuck do you mean you could have been a lesbian?" he said, as he sat down on the ottoman in the living room and wiped his forehead. He had blood from the glass breaking on his shirt and he didn't even care. He knew within his heart he had done irreparable damage and nothing could, or would, change. I told him about the encounter with Mike and his wife, Nicole. He was amazed and couldn't believe that I went through with something like that, but I told him about the liquor and how that influenced my decision to go through with it.

"I wish I had known you were curious. I'd have found us a cutie to do it with," he said, with a little chuckle ,trying to break the tension. But, it didn't work at all.

I looked at him in rage and, just when I had something to say, my phone rang. The ringtone was Usher's *There Goes My Baby* and it was Malik. He uploaded that song to my phone one night when I was asleep and I never removed it. I always hoped one day to find a man that truly loved me, just for me, no matter what. I know I was not an easy person to get along with.

"Hey!" I said, trying to sound as normal as possible.

"Baby, are you okay? I didn't hear from you all morning and I know we had it out a little. I don't want to argue with you. I love you. Where are you?" Malik said, sounding concerned about me.

"I'm okay. I just went to handle some business and look at some office space and also check with the realtor about the home sale," I said, glancing at Quincy.

"I'm okay. I made an appointment and I wanted you to go with me if you could this week. We'll talk about it later, but I'm fine," I said, forgetting that Quincy didn't know that I could be pregnant with his child. I looked over at him and he smirked at me, knowing that he could have sex with me if I was because I was already pregnant. He knew what my pussy felt like when I was and enjoyed the feeling. He quickly realized that I was speaking to Malik, his former best friend. All hints of desire disappeared when he put two and two together to know that I was fucking his friend, and in a relationship with him.

"Wait, that was 'Lik? You're fuckin' my nig? My best fuckin' friend? Are you serious, Tamika?"

The vicious temper that brought us to this fateful place was beginning to surface and I was regretting coming here to talk to him. A public place was indeed a safer place to have met him, since he had put his hands on me before.

"Yes, Quincy. You might as well know. There's a good chance that I am pregnant and it could either be yours or Malik's. I will be going to the doctor this week to confirm dates of conception and, when it's born, I'll do a test," I said, sounding as if it's a business transaction.

"You're going to keep this child? You don't even know whose child it is! Wow! I didn't know you were such a dusty bitch!" Quincy said, walking away to get a drink of Hennessy Black.

I was taken aback by his accusation, and responded with much anger to hurt him.

"Yes, you stupid son of a bitch! I'm keeping this child. I don't give a fuck if it's yours or Malik's. It's MY baby! You have three with Rachelle! Why can't I have something that belongs to me? Your dick wasn't even mine! It belonged to her, her, and her over there! So, please, don't try to get on me about my child. You didn't care enough to want a family with me. You just fucked for the hell of it, and what happened, happened. Lanai was a precious accident that turned into a lost blessing. I miss her so damned much and, right now, Malik and I are building a relationship. He loves me and that's what matters to me. Fuck you and fuck your feelings!"

I walked away and approached the front door. I'd had enough of dealing with his bullshit, and didn't even want to deal with him, but I gave him the benefit of the doubt. I was tired of it and he knew it, because I saw him walk towards me.

"Tamika, you're still bleeding! Let me get you something for that. "

He went to get something to stop my hands from bleeding and we sat and talked about the things that occurred and why. I was still upset about things, but this might have to be the best way to let them out, aside from killing him. I loved Quincy for who he was, but not for who he had become. That man had died along with Lanai and it took her death to show me just who he was. It's amazing how we can love someone for so long and still not know them.

"What possessed you that night?" Quincy asked me, referring to when I almost beat the shit out of his girlfriend, Veronica, and then came home and had crazy, wild, and passionate sex. All of this reminiscing caused us to be a little civil toward one another, and I had sat down and placed my head in his lap. He tore off his wife beater and wrapped it around my hand to stop the bleeding. I didn't cut a major artery but it was rather sore. It felt like a damned paper cut and it burned like hell!

"I don't know, Q. " I was honest in that. I didn't know what had possessed me. I didn't know what possessed me to do a lot of the things I did, but I knew that it would be to my advantage. At least, I believed so. I guess it was love. Love makes one do crazy things. Some people have no idea!

Bound By Lies

IF LOVING YOU IS WRONG

"Tamika, I'm not going to argue with you anymore. We've both had enough. Here are the divorce papers so we can both move on from this. I've loved you as best I could, and you have moved on, obviously. They are signed and please be careful when you open the envelope, because my wedding band is in there. "

I stopped short from walking out the door when he said this. I looked at him and opened the medium-sized manila envelope that so conveniently held the beginning of the rest of my life. I held the top open to avoid paper cuts since my hands were still sore from the glass earlier. In that envelope,I pulled out the platinum wedding band I purchased for our wedding. We made an agreement that we would purchase each other's jewelry and have it personalized. In my band, I had *Q's 4EverLuv* and in his, I had engraved *MidniteLuv4Eva.*

I pulled out the paperwork enclosed and it was signed divorce papers. All I needed to do was submit them to my attorney and it would be over. I loved Quincy, but not what we had become, and that was the worst part. I knew I would never not love him anymore and he would forever be a part of my life in some way, shape, or form but, for now... Right now, I needed to live my life according to me and quit selling myself short.

I walked over to Quincy, kissed him gently on the lips, and whispered in his ear, "thank you, baby boy". I could see the tears well up in his eyes. It was finally over for us and we could move on, or so we believed.

Later on that week, I went to my scheduled appointment at the doctor to determine how far along I was. I wasn't feeling like myself at all, and while both Quincy and Malik wanted to accompany me, I decided at the last minute to go alone and would let them know what happened after.

I always hated doctors' offices, especially after Lanai passed away. I didn't make an effort to get dressed up to see the doctor and simply had on some a white tee-shirt, dark grey sweats, and silver and grey Nike sneakers. Fashion was definitely not a priority today and it showed. I was casual, but focused on getting what I needed done. I walked into the building that would hold my fate and exhaled. It seemed as if I was holding my breath forever.

"Good morning," I said to the receptionist at the front desk. "I am Tamika Adams-Thompson, and I have an appointment to confirm pregnancy. "

She looked at me and smiled, seemingly loving her job, whereas I didn't know how to feel with regards to my pregnancy, especially not knowing who the father was. I gave a weak smile and took the forms she handed to me on a clipboard, after confirming my name and appointment time.

"Have a seat, Mrs. Thompson. The doctor will be with you shortly," she said, in a cheerful tone as if she just found a cure for a terminal illness. Her happiness was nauseating and I began to feel a wave of it as I stood in front of her.

"Thank you. Can you direct me the bathroom, please? I'm feeling a little nauseous. " I was accustomed to this feeling since I'd had it before, but this was stronger than I've ever experienced.

"Sure, it's around the hall to your left, and here's something to get a urine sample as well, since you will be in there. " This chick was really pushing it, but I obliged so as not to irritate myself anymore. I wasn't in the mood to pee in a cup, but I guess they wanted to make sure things were accurate. I took the cup and replied simply, "thank you".

Five minutes later, I returned, handed the receptionist my cup, and went to take a seat to wait for my name to be called. I picked up a magazine from a table to read, and gazed around. There were a lot of couples in the waiting area, anxiously anticipating news of an arrival. I nervously smiled at one couple, whose glance I kept, and grabbed my ring finger, only then realizing it was still bare. I silently wished that I had someone there with me but that wasn't possible, not given my circumstance.

I decided to check some emails and I noticed one from Trevor. I still needed to contact him regarding the proposal he gave me a few months ago. This email seemed more personal and I gave myself a mental note to give him a call in a few days when I felt more up to it. I wanted things to be casual with him and I knew he still has feelings for me.

"Tamika Thompson! Tamika Thompson!" I heard the nurse call out my name. I don't know how long I had been waiting, but hearing my name startled me out of my thoughts. The magazine I was reading no longer held my interest and I sighed and began to walk slowly to the examination room.

"Please step into Exam Room #2 and get undressed, leaving just your underwear on, until the doctor arrives. She will be with you shortly to talk to you about the results of your urine test that you took. " She seemed to know something that I didn't, but it wasn't something I didn't already know since I had been down the road before. I quickly removed the clothing, leaving on my socks, and hopped up on the examination table. *It's always so cold in the room*, I thought to myself.

I looked around and smiled half-heartedly, touching my stomach without realizing it. I noticed a poster on the wall, detailing the month-by-month development of pregnancy. I knew I was in the early stages and began to get excited at possibly expecting again. Sadly, memories went back to Quincy and all that went on during that crazy time, but I am determined not to let my past determine by future. Just then, the doctor entered the room to tell me my fate.

"Mrs. Thompson, how are you today?" she said, as she was taking notes in my file. She continued to ask about my medical history, which hadn't changed much since Lanai, and I updated her. I hated going through the logistics and only answered some questions, because I knew the procedure and it was the only way to move on to another topic.

"...after reviewing the urine sample, as well as the examination we've given you today, your HCG levels determine that you are, indeed, pregnant and you are about seven weeks, which means that the baby was conceived..."the doctor said, but I was too focused on the dates to hear anything else. I know exactly when that was. It was when Quincy and I made love and then the day after Malik and I did.

I hopped off the table and began to throw up in the garbage can next to the door. I, all of a sudden, felt so nauseous and I couldn't control it.

"I'm so sorry, Doctor! I just felt so very ill. I guess it's morning sickness," I said, as I gathered my clothes, preparing to re-dress.

"Tamika, are you okay? Why are you getting dressed? We haven't discussed your options. I can provide you with information regarding support for you," she said, with a puzzled look on her face.

I darted out of the office like a bat out of hell. It was confirmed that I was pregnant, but I was still unsure that the baby was Malik's or Quincy's. I didn't know what to do but I was going to call Malik, and we were going to be happy no matter what.

Bound By Lies

TOO CLOSE FOR COMFORT

I ran out of the doctor's office and into the parking lot. I threw my Blackberry unto the passenger seat and broke down in a barrage of tears. *I am pregnant*, I thought to myself. All I cared about was that I was having another baby. I grabbed my Blackberry and started to dial Quincy's number. It rang once and hung up. What the fuck was I doing? Why was I calling my ex-husband? I regained my composure and dialed numbers on my phone once again. I had to let him know what the results were.

"Hello," he said. It felt so awkward, but I had to let him know I was sorry how things were, and how much I loved him.

"Malik! Hey! I'm happy I caught you. Are you busy? I'm at the doctor and I got the results of the pregnancy test. "

"Hey, Tee. No, I was just laying here and, coincidentally, looking at some pictures of us in my phone. How are you? You sounded funny when I spoke to you the other day," he said, sounding sexy and sleepy at the same time.

"Baby, I miss you! I'm coming over, but I need to handle the sale of the house. I want it done soon, so we can begin OUR life together. So much has happened and I want it to be all about us from now on," I told him, hoping he was now convinced that I wanted to be with him. I had to show him that it was all about us and our family.

"No need to come out here. You've spent way too much time in Brooklyn as it is. I'll come out there and help you pack and get things situated. I want to see you, anyway. I'll be there around six and I'll bring dinner. "

I was grinning into the phone when he said that and I know he felt it. The rapport we had was filled with passion, love, and something fresh. I was in love again and, damn ,it felt good.

"Okay, baby, I'll see you later. I love you!" It felt so good to finally say it.

"See ya' later, Tee," Malik said, and then hung up. It felt kinda weird that he didn't respond to what I said, but I didn't think anything of it. I know how we left things the other day wasn't really good, so he was just being cautious, I surmised.

I got in the truck and began my trek to Westchester, New York, where my life would change, once again, in a few months, and I would be home in Brooklyn, where my heart belonged. The ride on I-95 had me thinking of so many things and I couldn't wait to tell my parents about the baby. That would help mend things between us and my mother would love me, and especially Malik, again. I know how she felt about Quincy and I breaking up and I just wanted things right. I must have been speeding because I pulled up to the driveway rather quickly and got a crazy feeling in my stomach. The last time that happened there was trouble and, once again, my senses were correct.

As I put my car in park and observed my home, I noticed that something looked strange. I placed my keys in my hand and my phone in the other, ready to dial the police if I needed to. I looked at my door and it was unlocked, even though I knew I locked it. *Maybe it's Malik, surprising me*, I thought. I was so used to things being crazy since Quincy's drama that I was on guard with everything.

I looked around and I didn't see anything, but I looked down and I saw rose petals. There was a trail of rose petals all the way from the floor to the stairs leading to my bedroom. Malik was definitely here and he was making it so much easier to love him.

"Malik! Baby! Are you here?" I yelled, as I dropped my purse on the couch and ran up the stairs. I was getting excited at seeing the prospect of the man I loved doing something so romantic. I'm sure he knew of what the results of the pregnancy was and wanted us to celebrate.

I followed the red rose petals to my bedroom door and opened it. It was dark, with lights illuminating my bed, and there were a multitude of roses all over the bed. I smiled and saw a figure lying down on the bed.

"Malik! Baby, is that you?" I was ready to begin making up, and making love to my man, and stripped at the base of the bed throwing my clothes wherever they landed. I was down to my bra and panties and walked over to the side of the bed, pulling back the covers. What I saw caused me to scream a blood curdling scream and pass out. When I awoke, I was in my living room, waiting for the police, with a severe headache.

"Who the fuck would do something like this? I am devastated! I feel like I've been violated!" I said, taking a sip of water and adjusting my satin robe around my breasts. It didn't matter who it was anymore; I didn't want anyone to get too close to me because, as soon as they do, trouble comes to find me.

"I don't know, but are you okay? You really should have called me and not went in the house," Quincy said. He happened to stop by the house to see if the paperwork was signed for the divorce, to collect some more things, as well as drop off the key, since he failed to do that when I saw him, and had found me on the floor in the bedroom. He almost didn't come in when he saw the rose petals, but because he knows I don't like them anymore, he knew something was wrong.

"Q, I'll be fine. When are the police coming? I need to clean up and just leave. This house is nothing but a bad omen now. Who would kill Trevor? My ex and have him in my bed? Is that what your bullshit has come to? People getting killed around me to send a fucking lesson?" I got up to walk and began to feel a little woozy.

"Tamika, sit your ass down! I'm not even supposed to be here, so calm down, because I don't want to look like I'm doing something against the orders. "

Just then, the door opened and it was Malik. The icy stare between the both of them was colder than being in the waters that sunk the Titanic. I jumped up and ran over to him and he caught me, smothering my face with kisses. Quincy stood up, walked over to Malik with a nod, and walked out.

"Quincy? You can't leave! You have to give the police an account of what you saw! Please!" I practically begged him to stay but he wouldn't budge.

"Your account is all you need to give them. "He placed the house keys in my hand and kissed me on the cheek leaving. I knew he would be back but, right now, it was too much to see his ex-wife and best friend together.

"Tamika, come tell me what happened, please," Malik placed his arm around my waist and held me close.

"Malik, I have to recount the same fucking story to the police. Can't I just wait 'til they come?"

"No, I want to know what happened so that I can," he was interrupted by a knock at the door. It was Westchester Police coming to see my home, which is now a crime scene.

"Mrs. Thompson? May we come in?" one of them said. I caught the nametag, and it was Carmona.

"Yes, I'm here. Please come in. Everything happened upstairs, it seems. "I didn't want to go back upstairs, so I was willing to do what I needed to do to avoid it.

I looked over at Malik and he was clueless on how to react to this uncomfortable situation, but kept his cool. Officer Carmona spoke to her partner and directed him upstairs.

"Just follow the trail of roses, I guess. I'm gonna call a bus to take Mrs. Thompson to get some medical attention. We need forensics and the morgue to check out the body," she said, taking out a pen and paper to begin taking notes.

"Whenever you are ready to begin, Mrs. Thompson," Officer Carmona said, taking one more look at my home, which has now become a murder scene. The damage was significant, but discreet, with the focal point being my bedroom. They clearly knew exactly what to do and I was worried that, this time around, the lies were catching up to me and this had nothing to do with Quincy.

"Mrs. Thompson! Please, whenever you feel comfortable enough to begin, I'd like to get the information so we can get you the help you need. Do you need protective custody? You can't stay here, as this is now a crime scene investigation. Is there anywhere you can stay?"

"She'll be staying with me from now on," Malik said, looking at me. He smiled, nervously seeking approval, but I know inside he was very uncomfortable and didn't know what changes this would cause to our relationship. We were moving rather fast, but we didn't know if it was going to help or hurt us.

"I'm ready now to begin," I said, wiping my face after receiving a hand squeeze from Malik. He was so very supportive, and I just want my nightmare to stop. This seemed never-ending, and didn't seem like it would be over anytime soon.

"I just came from the doctor and decided to come home, and Malik was supposed to meet me later today, so, I got here and I saw that the door was open. He has a key and I figured he wanted to surprise me earlier than we planned, and noticed the roses, which cemented that idea. I went upstairs and I saw the rose petals on the floor to my bedroom and opened the door. The candles were lit all over and I saw a figure lying in my bed," I said, describing what caused me to even venture upstairs. My palms began to sweat and I felt palpitations in my chest. This was getting to me and I was becoming overwhelmed with emotion.

"Ma'am! Are you okay?" Carmona turned to the officer keeping watch at the door, while forensics began to take pictures of the door, kitchen, and other important areas.

"Yes, I am okay. I am just feeling a little anxious about these details," I said, wanting to get it over with.

"I understand. Please continue," Officer Carmona said, as she waited for me to tell her what I saw that frightened me.

"Well, I stripped, like I said, and then walked over to the side of the bed, and saw a body lying there, and I thought it was Malik. I began to kiss the side of his face, but it felt weird, and not like him, so I stepped back and the mirror for my dresser caught my eye. It had something written on it in red lipstick and, when I read it, that's when I pulled back the covers to see my ex- fiancé, Trevor Cunningham, laid in my bed...dead, and with his penis severed and stuffed in his mouth. "

I began to cry all over again, recanting the events, and I shivered all over to know someone could be after me to kill me.

"Ma'am, I know this is difficult, but what did the writing on the mirror say? It's very important to determine who could be involved and who we can deem as a suspect," Officer Carmona said, ready to use my information as a clue to who could have made such a horrendous scene.

"They wrote with my red lipstick,

'You Can Run But You Can' t Hide, Bitch!!'"

I began to sob and Malik grabbed me, holding me close. He had no idea that my past was coming back to haunt me. I didn't know it would surface so soon, but I wanted to be safe and in his arms with this baby. This is where I would be if it was the last thing I did. As soon as I thought those words, I knew it would come back to haunt me!

"Well, ma'am, that's enough information right now to get things started. I am going to tell you to come with us to the hospital to get checked out. We want you to go somewhere after and then a detective will speak to a few people you have been in contact with the last few weeks and months," Officer Carmona said.

"Thank you, Officer, for helping us out. This is definitely a difficult time for both of us, and I just want her to be okay," Malik said, as he escorted her to the door. She gave him a crazy look and mouthed some words, but I didn't know what exactly she said. I just sat back on the couch, rubbing my stomach, which seemed to be rumbling with anxiety and also the baby inside.

"Sir, I am going to have to ask you to come down to the station without her and talk to me. We found some of your fingerprints on the bed, as well as on the mirror, and the story sounds a little suspicious to us, considering she didn't see you for a few days. Your fingerprints shouldn't be as prominent as they are," Officer Carmona said to Malik.

"No problem. I'll bring my attorney and we'll discuss further whatever is necessary to get this investigation underway," Malik said, as he took the business card from the cop. Malik fingered the business card, looked at the officer, and walked out of the house. I didn't know if he was coming back, but I felt like he would as we had unfinished business to tend to.

"Mrs. Thompson, we are all done here for now. The officers will allow you to gather some things so you may go with your friend. You are expected at the station in seventy-two hours and, please, don't let us come find you. Just call us and we will escort you. Given the nature of the crime, we just want to secure your safety," Officer

Carmona said, and left. Moments later, Malik reentered and walked over to me.

"Now that the bitch is gone, my question is why the fuck is that nigga in your bed? You fuckin' him?" He began to yell at me and his voice shook with anger.

"What the hell are you talking about, Malik? I told you and the officer what I found! You're trying to blame this bullshit on me? Malik, he's my ex, and he's DEAD. Why would you even think that I was having sex with him? I'm pregnant! You know what? Fuck you and fuck this situation! I'm getting my shit and I'm leaving. I don't need, nor want, your bullshit," I yelled back at him, running up the stairs. The medical examiner had placed so much tape around my bedroom, but I was able to grab a few things from my dresser. They left an officer there until I left.

"Is everything okay downstairs, ma'am?" the officer said, ready to go downstairs to diffuse the situation.

"I'm fine. I just want to grab a few things. As a matter of fact, I'll just grab my purse and leave and buy whatever I need. I'll see you in a few days and, please, call me for pick up. The plans have changed and I will not be staying with the gentleman downstairs. " I handed the cop my business card and promised to follow up with them. I bolted downstairs, out of the house, and got in my truck. Malik was sitting his car and kept calling me to come over. I looked at my phone once again and decided to answer it because it had been buzzing since I left the house.

"So, you're leaving me? Where are you going to go?" he asked me, with irritation in his voice.

"Malik, I'm pregnant. I can't deal with the stress. I want to be okay since I haven't been in a while. I'm going to have to go to the doctor and see about anxiety pills. My ex-fiancé was killed in my bed and... " I paused to think maybe it was Quincy. I was worried that my past with him was catching up with me.

"Yeah, Tamika, I don't understand what that nigga was doin' in your bed. Why? What does Quincy have to do with this?" Malik was beginning to sound suspicious and I was getting nervous with the thoughts that were going through his head.

"Malik, I don't fucking know! When I was at the doctor, Trevor sent me a message saying he needed to talk to me and now he's gone! I don't understand what the fuck is going on and..."

Malik cut me off, yelling at me once again.

"Well,I need to know what the fuck is going on with you finding a nigga in your bed with a dick in his mouth! That's all I care about," he said.

All of a sudden, everything went dark and I felt myself sinking. I wasn't about to have another anxiety attack. I hadn't had one in a long time, even though with all that had taken place, I was due one. I placed my head on the steering wheel and closed my eyes, breathing in and out slowly. After a few moments, I hear tapping on my car window and I see it's Malik.

"Baby, open the door!" he says, grabbing the door handle.

TROUBLE DON'T LAST ALWAYS

Malik snatched the car door open to find me hysterically crying and losing consciousness. *Why must life always deal me these sets of cards? Am I truly meant to be happy?* I asked myself. He pulled me out of the vehicle and placed me in his car, which was parked not too far behind, giving me a bottle of water that he always keeps in his truck.

"Tamika, we have got to keep you safe. There's something going on and we don't know what it is. I don't want you hurt, especially since you are carrying my child," Malik said, with so much affection and caring ,it was hard to try to tell him the truth about the situation. I loved him more than anything, and I wanted him and I to work out and this would certainly change everything.

"Okay, Malik. I will relax. I need to go, though, to make sure I am safe. I need to go to my parents. They are where I need to be, because no one knows where I am. Maybe for a month, or so, would change things. Can I just go and relax? My mom would take care of me and my dad would love to see me. "

Malik looked at me with eyes that spoke of undying love and reached into his pocket, dropping to his knees.

"I wanted to give you this today but, with all the drama, I forgot. But, now seemed like no better time than any to show you how much I love you and want you in my life. " He pulled out a ring box and opened it. Inside was a two-carat, princess-cut, platinum, diamond engagement ring. I gasped and began to tear up at the sight of his romantic gesture.

"I know this isn't under the best circumstances, but do you think you would do me the honor of being my wife? I love you so much and I want to spend forever with you, no matter what the future brings. You have made me extremely happy and, I know we didn't begin this under the best circumstances, but I want you to love and be with me forever. I can't see myself with anyone else, and I want you to carry my last name. " Malik placed the ring on my left ring finger and asked, once again, officially, while down on one knee, "would you be my wife, now and forever?"

I was so shocked and jittery, yet I couldn't help but respond with tears in my eyes.

"YES! YES! I will love to be your wife, now and forever!" I said, grabbing him and kissing him seductively. He kissed my tears and told me he loved me.

"Malik, you know I still have to go to my parents to get my head together. I'm going to buy whatever clothes I need in Brooklyn and go back to work soon. It's been a while and I need to regain some normalcy in my life. I know I've said it time and time again, but things keep getting in the way"

"We'll work it out. You have some clothes at my house. I'm going to drop you off and then go to the police station to meet with the detective about the murder. She has to ask me questions about what I may or may not know. All I care about is you so we can begin our new life with our new baby."

I cringed when he said that, but I knew I had an appointment soon and would do what I needed to do in order to satisfy all questions. Malik got me into my car and followed me to his house in Brooklyn. I got myself some clothes, threw them in a bag, and also got myself cleaned up to go to my parents.

"So, you're gonna miss me when I go? I'll talk to you every day and, since you are closer, we can chill sometimes," I said, sounding like a little school girl.

"Of course, my darling! I'm going to miss my wife-to-be. I miss you already and you've not gone anywhere. I'm also going to miss my lil' princess that's growing inside of you," Malik said, as he rubbed my stomach that showed signs of a pouch already. His hands traveled lower and grazed my crotch to play with my pussy, beneath my skirt.

I already knew that he was feeling a little frisky and aroused, and I was, too, surprisingly. It had been a minute since he touched me, and that's what we'd planned before that harrowing experience back at my house. I missed him so much and I wanted him inside of me, as I felt my pussy throb, as his tongue invaded the crevices of my mouth. I walked him into his bedroom by his hand and stood in the middle of the bedroom floor. I started to remove his clothing and, with each kiss, a button was opened.

He sighed heavily as my fingers grazed his naked, muscular chest. My French manicured nails tickled him slowly as I reached the end of his button-down shirt. I pulled it off his shoulders and let it fall casually to the floor. Neatness wasn't a priority tonight. He grasped my tiny waist with his manly hands and pulled me closer, allowing his growing erection to lay comfortably on my thighs. With all the shit that's been going on, it was time for us to make love again.

I missed him and, even though I just got dressed to leave, Malik was making it very hard to not get undressed. I wore four-inch stilettos and, finally, we saw eye to eye. His brown eyes stared seductively at me knowing this was more than undressing him. This was removing all feelings of uncertainty I had for him. He caught a glimpse of my cleavage and decided it was my turn.

While I began at the top, he favored the bottom, and he sat me down on the bed and placed my feet on his lap. He examined my shoes carefully and removed them. His fingers touched and massaged my toes, carefully examining them for flaws. They seemed perfect in his eyes and he kissed them ever so gently, placing each toe in his mouth.

I giggled softly and lay back on the bed. His hand trickled up my thigh to the lower back and he removed the snap on my skirt. Grabbing me by the hand, he pulled me off the bed and I stood in front of him. As soon as I did that, my skirt fell to the floor and all that was left to be seen were my black, lace boy shorts that sat comfortably on my round, apple-shaped bottom.

I looked into his eyes and kissed him passionately, as our tongues danced a tune never heard by the human ear. My hands traveled below his waist to remove his slacks that were hiding an erection poking out from his boxers. He wanted me as much as I wanted him.

I laid him down, onto the bed, and removed my panties, straddling his dick slowly. He grabbed my waist and stopped me. "I'm not hurting the baby, am I?" he said.

"No, sweetie! We are just fine," I responded, and began to ride my dick. Malik grunted and kissed me passionately, and thrust his thunder into my canal, causing me to feel like I was floating. I had to tell him to slow down and he flipped me onto my side and placed my right leg on his left shoulder, thrusting into me while playing with my nipples that were erect.

"Oh, my God! I love you so much and will do anything to keep you! Tamika, you better not fucking cheat on me! This is my pussy!" Malik said. I felt weird even acknowledging those statements, but just said, "yes, baby!"

Those statements would come back to me sooner than I presumed at the moment.

"Tamika, this is my pussy, right! Ugh," he said, while grunting. I knew he was about to blow his load. It had been a while and my pussy was so wet from penetration. He flipped me onto my back and began to stroke me slowly, making love to my pussy until it began to curve to his dick. I creamed all over it and felt it throbbing, while he stopped and looked into my eyes.

"I love you, Tamika," he said, with tears in his eyes.

"I love you, too, Malik," and, the truth of it was, I always did but never said anything.

Malik continued to pound my pussy until he erupted his love juice inside of me, and we both collapsed in lustful slumber. When I awoke, Malik was gone, but left a note.

Hey! Going to see the detective about the case. I will be back later. Love Ya

Well, that was simple, I thought to myself and rolled back over. This pregnancy was taking all of my energy this time around and, hopefully, I'll be able to rest. I figured Malik would wake me when he came back from the meeting with the detective and I had no idea of what would be occurring in my absence.

AT THE POLICE STATION

Officer Carmona received a call from the desk officer and was told that Malik was waiting in the stationhouse to be seen. She knew she wanted Malik the moment she saw him, and was told about him from her girlfriend, Jazmine, that he was hot. She was bisexual, but, of course, she loved her some chocolate brothers and, while Jazmine was the male counterpart in the relationship, she let her do her thing and seek out sex from outside sources.

She had been watching Malik, Quincy, and Tamika for quite a while and knew that Malik and Quincy were best friends and had been wanting him for a long time. She felt bad that Lanai was in the crossfire of the vehicle she was driving, but made it her business to keep an eye on him and Tamika. Ever since that club incident where Tamika beat that woman's head in, she's been watching them and with good reason, since Tamika was out of control that night. She knew everything about each one of them and was even there when Rachelle and she fought earlier on. She was the one that gave Rachelle the address to her house in Greenburgh when they moved, but what she didn't know was that she would not have the baby and that Lanai would die in the process. Because of that, she tried to rectify the situation as best as she could in order to benefit everyone

Rebekah knew that all paths would cross and it happened just as she suspected. She was off duty while at the hospital when she saw the altercation between Quincy and Tamika. She tried to convince Tamika to file a complaint after the assault, but she didn't comply. She knew she would see her eventually, but she didn't know that she would link up with her man much sooner. Tamika was too hell bent on trying to find out about Quincy's cheating ways that she failed to realize that she's got some skeletons in her closet, as well. Either one of them would do fine: Quincy or Malik. She wanted to get Tamika back for something that would be revealed soon enough. She knew within her heart who murdered Trevor, but couldn't reveal it until she knew for sure. Her own ulterior motives would interfere with her duty as a police officer.

When she was called to the house, Rebekah was unsure if she should even respond, but, as an officer of the law and since it was in her sector, she was obligated to take the call. She was shocked with what she saw, but decided it was a sign that she would be able to get much closer to them both. After all, Jazmine did say that Tamika was fine as hell, and she always believed in killing two birds with one stone!

"Malik! Afternoon! I am Officer Carmona! I'd like to ask you a few questions about the night in question. Would you like some coffee?" she asked, trying to sound pleasant, yet professional. She knew the fine art of interrogation, and how to get what she wanted.

"Not a problem, ma'am. I just want to make sure things are taken care of and my fiancé's wellbeing is secure," Malik said, taking a seat and taking a cup of coffee from the officer.

"So, let's just get things underway, shall we?" Officer Carmona took out a recorder and pushed the button to journal all information regarding the night Trevor was murdered.

"Where were you that night? Did you and Mrs. Thompson have an argument?"

Malik shifted in the seat and remembered the discussion they had before she went to the house.

"Yes, we had a misunderstanding, but that's why I was supposed to meet her at the house. We were gonna make up and make things right, especially with the baby and all. I want us to be perfect, or damn near," he said, smiling.

A baby! she thought to herself. This will definitely get interesting!

"Oh, well, I guess a congratulations is in order. I wish you both well," Officer Carmona said to herself, while concocting a sinister plan. She already knew that Quincy and Tamika were married and obviously fucking. She needed to find out for herself whose baby it was. What she didn't know was that was the question of the century.

Officer Carmona and Malik concluded their interview and she received more than enough information, including the fact that they are engaged, Tamika is now living in Brooklyn, and her divorce with Quincy is final. She also discovered that she's pregnant and selling the house in Greenburgh. All that information would be pertinent to her plan to get Malik for herself. Her plan will be set into motion very soon, but it would do more harm than good, as she would discover once the betrayals unfold.

Bound By Lies

EIGHT WEEKS LATER

Living in Brooklyn, close to Malik and my parents, has been so good to me. I've been eating, resting, and working, and all things have come together for good. This baby, who I'm convinced is a boy, has been giving me a run for my money with morning sickness. I already had my appointment with my doctor and had an amniocentesis to make sure that the baby was healthy. As a woman in my thirties, I couldn't be too sure, especially since I had some issues with stress during my pregnancy with Lanai.

Just as I was rubbing my belly and thinking about my new and impending bout with motherhood, my Blackberry rings and it's my doctor.

"Mrs. Thompson?" the doctor's office says, and my heart begins to flutter.

"Yes?" I say, wondering what the urgency is.

"We need you to come in right away. We have the results of the amniocentesis. "

"Oh, okay, great. I'd like to make an appointment for some time next week to review it, and also have my sonogram," I say, sounding a bit relieved

"No, ma'am. I'm sorry, but you need to come in tomorrow. We also have the results of the prenatal DNA test you requested. There's something that needs to be discussed regarding the babies and their paternity. "

All of a sudden, I got woozy and yelled into the phone, "BABIES!"

THE END...or is it?

Illuminnessence Publishing presents

"BitterSweet"

Coming Summer/Fall 2011

Pick up the book that started it all…

Broken Promises Never Mend

Available on Amazon, Barnes and Noble,

and www. illuminnessencepublishing. com